TO LIVE IN TWO WORLDS

▲▲▲▲▲▲▲▲▲▲▲▲▲▲▲▲▲▲▲▲▲

To Live in Two Worlds

American Indian Youth Today

▼▼▼▼▼▼▼▼▼▼▼▼▼▼▼▼▼▼▼▼▼

Brent Ashabranner

Photographs by
Paul Conklin

DODD, MEAD & COMPANY

New York

1 2 3 4 5 6 7 8 9 10

Library of Congress Cataloging in Publication Data

Ashabranner, Brent K., 1921—
   To live in two worlds.

   Includes index.
   1. Indians of North America—Youth—Biography—Juvenile
literature.   2. Indians of North America—Social conditions—
Juvenile literature.   3. Indians of North America—Ethnic identity—
Juvenile literature.   I. Title.
E98.Y68A74   1984   305.2'3'08997073   83-25405
ISBN 0-396-08321-8

This book is for Eva Mae and Jerry

CONTENTS

TO LIVE IN TWO WORLDS

An Indian high school graduate poses with her proud parents following commencement in Oklahoma.

1

"Our Youth Are Our Future"

BEFORE THE COMING of Europeans, the Indian population of what is now the continental United States was about 2.5 million. By the close of the nineteenth century, their number had diminished to less than 250,000, and Indians were thought to be a people on the road to extinction because of wars, disease, and loss of their traditional homelands to white settlers.

Today about 1.5 million Indians live in this country, and no longer are they spoken of as the Vanishing Americans. Although Indians still make up less than one percent of the U.S. population, they have become one of the fastest growing ethnic groups in the country.

"Indians have refused to die out," a Cheyenne leader said recently. "We have survived. And Indians are going to have a future in this country because of our young people."

"Our youth are our future," says a publication of the Council of Energy Resource Tribes, an important Indian organization concerned with development of mineral reserves on reservations.

How do young Indian men and women themselves feel about the future that their tribal elders speak of? What is important to them? What do they want to accomplish? What special problems do they face in the America of the 1980s? What opportunities are open to them? To try to find answers to those questions and others, Paul Conklin, my photographer-colleague, and I traveled more than fifteen thousand miles to talk with young Indians on reservations and in cities and towns in many of the states with large Indian populations. For our purposes, young meant anyone of high school or college age and anyone getting started in a career.

We found no easy answers, nor did we expect to. We did find that most of the young Indian men and women we met talked openly once they were convinced that we really wanted to listen.

We spent one lovely spring afternoon sitting outdoors talking with students at the College of Ganado, a tiny educational oasis on the Navajo Reservation in Arizona where a two-year Associate Degree is offered. It was our introduction to the slang of Indian college students. They seemed to divide the Indian world into those who lived on reservations and those who did not. The reservation dwellers were "res" Indians. Those who had left the reservation to work and live in cities or urban areas were "urbies."

The students talked about "apples," Indians who thought like or wanted to be like white people. They are red on the outside but white under the skin. Apples, we were told, could be found on the res, but they were much more likely to be urbies. I asked what made an Indian become an apple.

"They're mostly older people," a boy named Kevin said, "people of our mothers' and fathers' generation or older. A lot

College of Ganado campus on the Navajo Reservation in Arizona

Poverty is apparent on much of the Indian lands. Here is the Rosebud Sioux Reservation in South Dakota.

A reflective Indian student at Arizona State University in Tempe

of them grew up being ashamed of being Indians. They got the idea in school that everything Indian was bad and everything white was good."

"And your generation has gotten rid of those ideas?" I asked.

"They're changing," Kevin said. "There are still a lot of kids on reservations who think they can't do anything just because they're Indians. But that's changing. I don't think that most Indians in college now have that hang-up."

The talk turned to why young Indians leave their reservations today, and everyone agreed that by far the main reason was to get away from the grinding poverty that blankets almost all Indian lands. "There aren't half enough jobs on reservations," someone said, "so people go to the cities looking for work. But most of them don't have any training, so what kind of jobs can they find there?"

This clearly was a subject that the students had done much talking about among themselves. They were taking courses in American Indian history and politics and were learning things that few of them had ever had a chance to learn in the high schools they came from. They knew that Indians are at the very bottom of the U.S. economic ladder. They knew that they have the highest unemployment and the lowest average income of any minority group in America.

"Is that why you're at the College of Ganado?" I asked. "So that you can get an education that will help you get away from the reservation?"

"I don't think we want to leave our reservations," said a Navajo student. "I know I don't. But I won't stay if I can't get a job here, and if I do have to leave, I want to do the best I can on the outside. That's why I'm at Ganado and that's why I'm going to the University of Arizona after I finish the two years here." He thought for a moment and added, "But I would come back to the reservation if I could get a job here. At least that's what I think now."

There was general agreement with the Navajo student's statement, but one girl said, almost to herself, "Everybody says they will come back, but how many really do?"

"Yes," I said, echoing her thought. "Half of the Indians in America today don't live on reservations."

"A lot of Indians don't have any reservations to live on," said a pretty girl dressed in jeans and a T-shirt. A beaded headband contained her long black hair. "There are over thirty Indian tribes in Oklahoma with no reservations. Their lands were all taken away by 'treaties' or broken up into individual allotments by the government."

I knew the history of Indian land loss, and I also knew that

A young Navajo

tribes without a land base had found survival particularly diffi-cult. That included most tribes in the eastern part of America.

I turned the conversation to the question of why a young Indian today would want to stay on a reservation where oppor-tunities are so limited and where—as I knew and as the stu-dents reminded me—living could be tough: poor housing, bad heating, outdoor toilets, few telephones, to name only some of the problems. I sensed that this was a subject they felt deeply about, but it took them a while to express their feelings.

One boy said, "If you've been raised on a reservation, if you are a Cheyenne or a Sioux or a Crow, you have your own world that's not like it is anywhere else. If you leave it, you remember it and miss it."

"What do you miss?" I asked.

The Navajo student said, "I went to school in Salt Lake City for a few years. You miss being with your people. You miss hearing Navajo spoken. You miss going to a healing ceremony or a squaw dance."

Someone else said, "You miss the Indian things—the hand games, the giveaways, the horse races, the powwows."

"I'm a San Ildefonso Pueblo Indian," said a student named James, "but my parents moved to Los Angeles when I was a year old and I lived there until I was thirteen. The school I went to was full of Spanish Americans, and that's what just about everybody thought I was. I knew I was an Indian, but I didn't think much about it. It didn't mean much to me. My grandmother lived with us, and she told me stories about our tribe and about life in the pueblo. I liked to hear the stories, but it was just like reading something out of a book. The stories didn't have anything to do with me.

"Then we moved back to New Mexico and lived in the pueblo. It was like another world, and I felt out of place there. But my folks were there and my grandmother, and the stories she had told me made things a little easier to understand. I started to learn our ceremonies and dances. I learned about our religion and tribal government. I learned our history, about how we had fought for five hundred years to keep our land. Little by little I became a part of the pueblo. Then one day it just hit me out of the blue. I'm an Indian. I'm a San Ildefonso Indian, and I have a very special culture. It made me feel good."

After a while the subject of prejudice came up, and it was clear that the students who lived on reservations had come up against it in nearby towns. "You go into a store or a restaurant and you just know you are going to be waited on last," someone said, "and you see a clerk watching you like he expects you to steal everything in sight."

"I never felt any prejudice in Los Angeles," James said, "but when we moved back to New Mexico I did. The high school I went to was not in the pueblo and it had mostly Anglo and Mexican-American students. Some of the teachers—not all of them but some—seemed to think that all Indian students were 'slow learners.' That's what I heard them call it but they meant dumb or stupid. And most of the non-Indian students didn't seem to know we were there."

An Apache student from the San Carlos Reservation in Arizona said, "A lot of people who live near reservations have grown up with the idea that all Indians are alcoholics, lazy, and unreliable. You call that stereotypes, don't you? They think they're lazy because they don't have jobs. I could take them out to the San Carlos Reservation and show them men and women digging little pieces of green stone—peridots—out of a rock cliff. It takes them all day in the hot sun to fill a can, and they sell a canful for four or five dollars to the jewelry makers. You call that lazy?"

"And if an Indian working in a town wants time off from his job to attend a sacred ceremony on the reservation, he's unreliable," someone said.

But on the subject of alcohol there was nothing but concern and unhappiness among the students. "It's our number one problem everywhere, I think," a girl said. "Older Indians drink because they live in poverty and can't cope with the white world. Young Indians drink because their elders do."

A boy from a Colorado tribe told a story. "I was going to high school in this town," he said, not giving the town a name, "and older men from my reservation would come into town and get drunk. A lot of them would go to sleep on the street.

A young member of the Ute Mountain Ute tribe in southern Colorado

You know, slouched up against a building. They all wore those black, high-crowned hats—they love them—and on weekends some kids from the high school would see how many hats they could steal from the drunks. One day at school a kid was bragging that he had stolen ten hats that weekend. I think he expected me to laugh like the others who were listening to him. Instead, I hit him. I was ashamed for my people, and that made me all the madder. I was suspended from school, but they let me back in after two weeks."

A girl said, "A friend of mine committed suicide when he was drunk. He was just nineteen."

What the girl said made me think of a talk I had had recently with a Cheyenne high school senior. He was back in school after spending two weeks in a teenage alcohol rehabilitation program. His hands shook and he seemed to be fighting to hold himself together. "I've been a drunk since I was thirteen," he said. "I'm trying to quit. I want to quit bad. But I don't know if I can."

Our conversation with the students at Ganado ended on a more cheerful note. "Do you think you are going to be able to cope with the outside world?" I asked them.

The student from Colorado laughed and seemed to speak for everyone when he said, "I think so. Do you think the outside world is ready to cope with us?"

IT WOULD BE unrealistic not to recognize that many young Indians in America are still disadvantaged by poverty, education that is often not appropriate, language difficulties, and a heritage of failure. But a new day truly has dawned. Propelled in part by the great civil rights movements of the late sixties and early seventies, many Indian tribes have demanded and are now receiving a stronger hand in the administration and

Young Indian rebel. He was one of a group of angry activists who took over BIA headquarters in Washington, D.C., for a week in the early 1970s.

development of their reservations and in planning the education of the young of the tribe.

Successful lobbying in Washington has created several federal scholarship programs to enable Indian high school graduates to go to college. In 1957 there were fifteen Indians enrolled at Arizona State University. In 1983 the Indian enrollment there was 550. Such dramatic increases have occurred at a number of other southwestern and western universities. Today more than forty thousand young Indians are enrolled in colleges throughout the country.

"Is the outside world ready to cope with us?"

The student at the College of Ganado had asked the question jokingly, but I thought about it many times as Paul and I talked with young Seminoles, Osages, Apaches, and Navajos from Arizona to Florida. A new generation of Native Americans has arrived, and they are determined to have their place in the mainstream of the country's life without severing their ancient tribal roots. It will not be easy for the government, the schools, and other Americans to understand that determination, but it is important that they do.

2

Lynn, a Navajo

MANY YOUNG INDIANS have strong feelings of inadequacy when they leave the reservation for the first time, usually to go to high school or college. They know little about the vast and strange non-Indian world, and they doubt their ability to succeed in it. Other conflicts develop. To be a success outside the reservation, will they have to forget the ways of their tribe? The following story of Lynn is unusual in some of its circumstances, but her thoughts, conflicts, and emotions are similar to those of thousands of young Indians when they step into the unfamiliar world that surrounds their reservation.

HER GROWING UP was no different from that of thousands of other Navajo children, except perhaps that her family moved around the reservation so much. But the family was small—just her mother, brother, and herself—so that made moving a

Two generations of Navajo women listen attentively at a tribal meeting in Arizona.

little easier. Lynn did not remember her father. He had left the family when she was an infant, and he never returned.

They moved often because they were poor, very poor, and had to stay with different members of her mother's family. But everyone was poor, so after they had stayed for a while with one of her mother's brothers or sisters, they would move someplace else so the burden would not be too great on one part of

the family. Lynn's mother tried to find work wherever they lived, but there were not many jobs on the reservation, especially for women.

It is the way of Navajo families to help family members in need, and Lynn never felt out of place or unwanted as she grew up. She played with her cousins and sometimes went with her brother into the desert when he herded sheep. There was always enough food to eat: mutton, corn, good Navajo fry bread, and sometimes, as a special treat, canned peaches from the trading post. A small suitcase held all her clothes, but there were enough to keep her warm in the cold winters.

Lynn was happiest when they stayed with her grandparents. They lived in a hogan, the traditional one-room Navajo dwelling made of logs and packed earth. It never seemed crowded despite extra people, and it was from her grandmother and grandfather that Lynn learned most about Navajo ways and beliefs.

She learned that the Navajo hogan is a home but also a holy place that must be built in the right way, just as the Holy People built the first hogans as examples for the Earth People. Before the hogan can be lived in, it must be blessed with songs from the blessing ceremony, and the door to every hogan must face east to catch the first light of the morning sun. In that way Changing Woman, the greatest of the Holy People, is honored. The sun was the father of Changing Woman's two sons, Monster Slayer and Born for the Water, and it was they who helped the Earth People in many ways.

On summer nights everyone slept outside the hogan, so that they could enjoy the soft breezes and the clean fresh air. Lynn would lie on her sheepskin and look up at the blanket of bright stars. Often as she drifted into sleep, she could hear the yipping bark of a coyote somewhere far off in the darkness, but she was not afraid.

Lynn went to school at four different places on the reservation, but moving around did not cause a learning problem for her. She had grown up speaking both Navajo and English, and her English improved quickly in school. She made top grades everyplace, and when she finished elementary school, she received a scholarship to go to a mission school in a large town off the reservation.

That was the beginning of a new life in a new world for

Navajos learn the skills of an auto mechanic at a school on the reservation in Arizona.

Here a Navajo learns the intricacies of electronic assembly at a plant on the Arizona reservation.

Lynn. It was a world that kept opening up, expanding, showing her new things. The school had a library with more books than she could imagine. Even though she was only in the ninth grade, her teachers made it clear to her that she was at the mission school because they knew she could be a good student, and they expected her to be one.

The town was by far the biggest place she had ever been in. There were supermarkets, department stores, restaurants, motels, theaters, and even bookstores. Sometimes on Saturday afternoons she would walk down the main street, just looking in the shop windows and wandering through the supermarkets. She had no money to buy things, but that did not matter.

At first she was very homesick for her family and friends on the reservation. Before going to the mission school she had never spent a single night away from her family. But all of the students at the school were Navajos from the reservation and that helped a great deal.

Lynn thought that she would be at the mission school until she graduated from high school, and it was a complete surprise when, about midway in the second term of her sophomore year, a group of her teachers asked her to come in for a conference. They told her about a new government program for finding minority high school students—blacks, Hispanics, American Indians—who showed unusual academic ability and sending them to some of the best college preparatory schools in America.

"We want you to try to win a place in the program," Lynn's teachers told her. "The competition will be very great, but we think you have a chance."

Lynn felt a small stab of fear. "If I am selected, where will I go?" she asked.

"We don't know," one of the teachers told her, "but most of the schools are in California and on the East Coast."

"That would be so far from the reservation," Lynn said.

Her teachers continued to talk to her over the following days, and they seemed so sure she should apply for the program that Lynn finally agreed to fill out the application papers and take the entrance examination. To herself she said, "I know I won't be selected, so there is nothing to worry about."

A short time later she took the entrance examination in

which she had to compete with all of the other minority students across the country who wanted to get into the program. She had never taken a test like that before, and she was sure that she had done miserably on it. She put it out of her mind and returned to her classwork and school life. The term was nearly over, and the thought of going back to the reservation made her happy.

And then one day she was called to the principal's office. He smiled when she walked in and he held up a piece of paper. "Congratulations, Lynn," he said. "You've been chosen! You're going to Brandermill School in Vermont." (At Lynn's request, the name of the school has been changed.)

Lynn would never forget the numb feeling in the pit of her stomach. "But it's so far away," she said.

"Well," the principal said, "Brandermill is one of the best college preparatory schools in the country. You're very lucky to be going there."

Yes, Lynn thought, she was lucky. She knew that. And she did want a good education. But why did she have to go so far away to get it? "Will I go in September?" she asked.

"That is one thing you may not like so well," the principal replied. "There's a special summer program at the University of Texas. You'll get courses in speed reading, English, and math, so that you will be better prepared for the fall term at Brandermill."

The numb feeling grew in Lynn's stomach. "Do I have to go?" she asked. "To the summer school, I mean?"

The principal smiled again. "I'm afraid you do," he said. "And you really need that work to get ready for the fall."

Lynn could feel the hurting at the back of her eyes, but she fought back the tears. "But I need to go home," she said.

"You can go home," the principal told her, "but not for a long visit. The summer program starts in June."

And that was the way it was. Instead of three months at

The Navajo Community College in Tsaile, Arizona, has used traditional tribal motifs in its architecture. In the foreground is a hogan, traditional home of the southwestern desert. In the background is a modern new administration building in which the hogan shape appears in glass.

home she would have two weeks. Two weeks to be with her family! On the bus ride from the school back to the reservation she sat in a window seat, and when they crossed into the reservation, she stared out at the red earth, at the huge bare rocks sculpted over thousands of centuries by wind and water into fantastic shapes. She stared at the awesome bulk of Black Mesa in the background and at the little patches of spring desert wild flowers along the roadside, tiny spots of purple, red, yellow, and white.

Lynn went to her grandparents' hogan, and her mother and brother came there so that they were all together. The two weeks passed like the flashing of pictures on a screen, and yet like pictures, some scenes stood still, and Lynn knew that she could carry them with her anywhere.

There were the times she would go with her grandfather for water. The hogan had no running water, and every few days he would drive his old pickup truck to a windmill down the road and fill two wooden barrels. Upon their return to the hogan, Lynn would help transfer the water from the barrels to containers inside and outside the house.

Some mornings Lynn would sit with her grandmother and help her grind corn for bread or mush. One morning as they worked, her grandmother explained again why grinding stones are so important. They were first brought to Navajos by the Holy People, she said, and women who learn to use them properly will be happy and healthy and even live longer. And the greasewood stirring sticks, if they are kept clean, will mean that a family will never be hungry. Hunger, which is really an evil spirit, thinks that the sticks are arrows which will kill it, so it stays away.

These were not the kinds of things that a person learned in school, Lynn thought, but she was glad that she knew about them. They were the teachings that her grandmother and her Navajo ancestors had lived by, and Lynn felt truth and meaning in them. Perhaps hunger was not an evil spirit, but it was bad, and it had less chance of getting into homes where women were happy and busy and knew how to prepare clean and nutritious food.

The day came too quickly when Lynn took a bus to Phoenix and boarded an airplane for the flight to Texas. She had never flown before and she was excited. She had thought she would be frightened, but she was so nervous thinking about the summer program that first-time flying fears couldn't crowd their way into her mind.

I'll bet I won't even get through the summer program, she thought, as she stared out of the plane window at the blur of ground below. I'll never make it to Vermont.

But it was not that way at all. When she reached the uni-

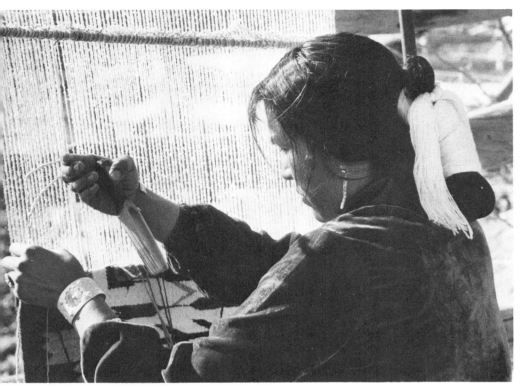

A Navajo woman weaves an intricate pattern in her rug.

versity, she was plunged into such a whirlwind of activity that she had no time to be frightened, uncertain, or even homesick. The program instructors pushed her and the other students into all-day classroom and laboratory sessions in mathematics, reading improvement, and English.

The teaching staff used methods and equipment that Lynn had never heard of, but after only a week she knew that she was reading faster and understanding more of what she read than she ever had before. She was pleased and excited by what was happening to her, and she was sure that she was doing well in the math program. English was the only problem. All her life she had spoken both English and Navajo, but sometimes, especially when she was under stress, she thought in Navajo. It was a problem she would just have to work out,

Lynn knew, and she was determined not to lose her Navajo language in solving it.

The other students in the program were a happy surprise for her. They were there because of their high test scores but also because they were from minority groups and poor families. They all wanted a good education.

These similarities made it easier for them to talk, to get to know each other, to relax together. After a hard day of classes, it was fun to get together in someone's room and talk about how they got to this place and what was happening to them here. On weekends when a group of them would go out for pizza or to a movie, it seemed to Lynn that she had known them for a long time.

Almost before she knew it, the summer program was over. She said her good-byes, some of them sad ones. She packed her suitcase and caught the plane for the East Coast.

She would never forget her first impressions of Brandermill: the huge old ivy-covered buildings, the beautifully landscaped campus still green at summer's end, the hundreds of cool, confident white-skinned girls walking in pairs, sitting on building steps in small groups, laughing and talking. It seemed to Lynn that they all had long blonde hair.

She learned some things about Brandermill before arriving. She knew that it was a prep school for the children of rich people. The tuition for one year was several thousand dollars, which was more money than Lynn could imagine. The school could afford to hire the very best teachers and it did. Brandermill's academic standards were the highest. Everyone had told Lynn how lucky she was to get to go to such a school.

But two weeks into the school term she was miserable. She was desperately lonely and homesick for her family and Navajo friends. She longed to see the red earth of the reservation, the great rocks, the sheltering bulk of Black Mesa. In the muggy

New England September, she could almost feel the crisp, clean Arizona air. The ache inside her was a physical thing.

And for the first time in her life Lynn knew what it meant to feel depressed. She sat silently in all her classes, afraid to speak up, feeling that she could not compete with her well-educated classmates. In literature class they talked about books and writers that she had never heard of but that everyone else seemed to know. Math had seemed easy; here at Brandermill it was suddenly hard. She was having problems with her written English. As the fall term wore on, Lynn was sure that she was failing.

And she made no friends. A few of the girls in her dorm talked briefly with her sometimes, usually about a class assignment, but no one made an effort to really get to know her. She did not make an effort either because she did not know how. She would have liked to know more about them, about how they lived, but they did not seem curious about her. Most of them had known each other from past years at Brandermill, and they were turned in on their friendships and little social groups. Lynn did not think that they were being deliberately unfriendly.

I'm not a part of their lives, so they just don't see me, Lynn thought. It's like I wasn't here.

By mid-October Lynn was sure that she should leave Brandermill and return to the reservation. She went to her counselor to tell him of her decision. He listened quietly as she explained that she was not making it in her classes and that she was unhappy with her life at the school.

"I'm a Navajo," she said, "and I should be back where I belong."

"You are a Navajo," her counselor replied, "and right now this is where you belong."

"But I'm failing," Lynn repeated.

Navajo country

"Only in your mind," the counselor said, "and we've got to change that. Have any of your teachers told you you're failing?"

"No," Lynn said. "I just know it."

The counselor smiled. "You just think you know it," he said. "I've been following your work. I've talked with all your teachers within the last week. You're doing okay in everything. You're doing well in history, in fact. Your written English needs work, but you're certainly not failing in English."

"But I'm not happy here," Lynn said.

"That's a different thing," the counselor said, "and that's why you think you're failing. What you are doing is about as hard to do as it can be. You have come out of a very special way of life into one that is entirely different. The people are different. The country is different. The school is different. There are very few people who could do what you're doing and succeed at it. That's why the selection board picked you. They believed you could do it."

"But I can't," Lynn said.

The counselor looked at her, "You can do it," he said. "When you first came here, I wasn't sure that you could, but now I am. If you leave school now and go back to the reservation, you won't feel good about yourself. You'll feel that you let down your tribe, your family, and your friends. You'll be sorry you left here. I don't want to put more pressure on you than you can handle, but I have to tell you what I think is the truth."

Lynn nodded but did not say anything.

"Look," her counselor said, "you hang on until Christmas break. You'll get to go home then. Dig in now. Mark off the days on a calendar. Do anything you have to do to stick it out. When you get home, back to the reservation, you can decide whether you want to come back to Brandermill or whether you can come back. That's the place to make the decision."

Somehow it became a little easier after her talk with the counselor. Lynn did not mark off days on the calendar. What she did was throw herself into her studies with fierce energy. She spent more time at the library, more time going over her assignments a second and even a third time. The hard work made the days slide by more quickly.

She forced herself to speak up in her classes, even literature class, and it pleased and excited her that more than once the teachers praised her answers. She began to talk a little more to the other girls in the dorm, and now and then someone stopped by her room just to chat.

But on the last day before the Christmas break her excitement at the thought of going home was almost more than she could bear, and the feeling continued throughout the long flight to Phoenix. Just as in the summer, she again would have two weeks with her family in Navajoland. Then in so short a time she would have to go back to Vermont. But suppose she decided not to return. She could spend the rest of her life on the reservation. Was that what she wanted? The thought left Lynn confused and curbed some of the excitement inside her.

That night Lynn sat with her mother and grandparents in their hogan and ate mutton stew, corn, and fry bread for the first time in months. A cold winter wind howled around the hogan, but it was warm inside. They sat by the fire, and Lynn told them about Brandermill, her courses, her teachers, the big beautiful buildings, her fine dormitory room.

"I never thought I would be in a school as grand as that," Lynn said, "but I would rather be here, right where I am now."

"This is your home," her grandfather said.

During her visit Lynn talked to her mother and grandmother about something that was troubling her greatly. "What if I turn into a white person?" she asked. "If I learn white ways and how they think, if I learn their language and read their books, if I spend most of my time with them—won't I become a white person?"

Her grandmother answered in Navajo and used the Navajo word for their tribe, *Dine*, which means "The People." "You should learn the ways of the white people," she said. "But the ways of The People are deep inside you. I do not think you will forget who you are."

And her mother said, "Nothing can make you a white person unless you want to be one."

In that moment Lynn's decision was made. She would return to Brandermill. On the day she left the reservation and flew east to begin her second term, Lynn said her good-byes sadly, but she felt a confidence she had not known before.

When she arrived at Brandermill, the great campus, the fine buildings, the blonde students did not frighten her. She knew what was ahead for her, and she knew now that she could do the work. Most important, she was sure she could do it and still be what she was and wanted to be, a Navajo.

LYNN'S STORY does not end at Brandermill, of course. She graduated with an excellent academic record and went on to take a degree from a good college. She returned to the Navajo Reservation to teach in an elementary school for several years. She now lives in Phoenix and works with an organization that arranges educational opportunities for Indian children.

Today Lynn moves easily and confidently in the non-Indian world, but she knows that, wherever she may be, her roots in the Navajo world are deep and secure.

▲▲▲▲▲▲▲▲▲▲▲▲▲▲▲▲▲▲

3

He Whose Children
Come Back to Him

BOUT ONE out of every two Indian students who
starts high school drops out before he graduates. That
rate is twice as high as for white students. Why does
this happen? There are several reasons that educational re-
searchers give. Language problems are one reason; many Indian children speak little or no English when they enter school,
and that learning handicap is hard to overcome. Extreme poverty is another reason. But a third reason, which some educa-
tors feel is the most serious, is the poor attitude that many
young Indians have about themselves, a poor self-image. What
it comes down to is that many Indian students quit school
simply because they think they can't do the work.

Leroy Falling knows a great deal about the self-image
problems of young Indians. As a Cherokee growing up in
Oklahoma, he experienced them firsthand. As a teacher in reservation schools for much of his life, Lee, as his friends call
him, saw how feelings of being inadequate profoundly affected

Lee Falling

the lives of his students. As an educational administrator in the Bureau of Indian Affairs, where he is now, he still works with the problem. Here Lee speaks for himself in describing his experiences with poor self-image and related problems of young Indians.

I KNOW YOU want me to talk about young Indians today and I will, but I'm going to talk about their parents, too, because you can trace back to the older generation a lot of what is going right and what is going wrong for Indian youth now. My wife and I have raised three sons and a daughter, so I know something about that.

You talk about a self-image problem. We really had one

when I was growing up in Oklahoma in the thirties. My folks had a farm in Craig County, which was once Cherokee Territory. The farm was 160 acres, the allotment my father got when the government broke up the land owned by the Cherokee Nation. We were poor, I mean really poor, but we raised enough food to feed the family and ran a few head of cattle, which gave us a little cash to buy things. I guess we were as well off as most people in those times.

I knew hardly anyone but other Cherokees, most of them my relatives, until I went to high school. I took my elementary grades in a school called Wolf School, which was on land donated by a Cherokee man with that name. We learned to read and write in English with some study in the Cherokee language as well. When I started high school I had to take the school bus to a town called Centralia. Most of the students in the high school were white, and all of the teachers were white, of course.

They didn't have separate public schools for Indians like they did for blacks in those days, but that doesn't mean there wasn't prejudice in the schools we went to. Indian kids seldom took part in class discussions, and teachers didn't bother to try to pull us in. They seldom called on us to answer questions. We were never called in for counseling about taking college preparatory courses. It was just assumed that Indians wouldn't go to college. If we didn't understand something, we waited until after class to see the teacher. Sometimes we took a note up because we were afraid to talk.

I think the main thing that kept us in school was sports. The Cherokee boys were often good athletes, so we were welcomed on the teams. My main sports were baseball and track, but I was on the high school basketball team too. I was short, but I must have been pretty good because I finally became a starter, and the starting five always played the whole game

The future of this nineteen-year-old Papago Indian does not seem bright. A high school dropout, he has no job and no job skills. He stands in front of the small adobe house he shares with his parents outside of Tucson.

unless someone fouled out or got hurt. The team just had five uniforms—those were Depression days, remember—and a player coming out of the game had to go to the locker room, take off his suit, and give it to the substitute. So the coach never made substitutions unless he had to.

Well, more about how Indian kids saw themselves through white people's eyes. I had four brothers and four sisters, just an average-sized Cherokee family in those days. For some reason, some kind of genetic throwback, I guess, my sister Betty Mae and I were several shades lighter in complexion than anyone else in the family. My father always called me his little white boy.

One day I was out with my brothers when a younger brother Fred cut his hand very badly in a freak accident. The blood was really pouring out, and we didn't have any idea of how to stop it. We used an old Cherokee remedy and it helped but not enough. We knew we had to act fast, so we piled in the old Model-T and drove to the nearest doctor. Fred was about gone by the time we arrived. The doctor took one look and told us to take him in his office. Then we waited outside for what seemed like hours. Finally the doctor came out and said Fred was going to be all right but that he was going to have to stay in bed for a while.

"But he might have died," the doctor said. He was really mad and he pointed a finger at me and yelled, "Why didn't you stop that bleeding?"

"None of us knew how to stop it," I said.

The doctor didn't know any of us, and he didn't even look at my brothers. He pointed his finger at me again and said, "*You* should have known how."

I realized then that the doctor thought I was white. He figured that was why I should know about stopping bleeding. He knew the other kids were Indians, and he didn't expect them to know anything. The doctor went back in his office and came out with a bottle of iodine and a swab stick. He made me strip down to my underwear, and he dabbed iodine all over my body on pressure points for stopping bleeding. Then he showed me how to apply a tourniquet. He never once looked at or said anything to my brothers. It was just like they didn't exist.

"And don't you ever forget," the doctor yelled at me as he went back into his office, slamming the door.

Later when we climbed back into the Model-T to go home, one of my brothers looked at me and grinned. "And don't you ever forget, white boy," he said.

I think it was that experience with the doctor more than anything else that made me decide to go to college. I don't remember how my reasoning went, but I'm sure it had something to do with thinking I could make it in college because I had white skin. That shows you how much our image of ourselves was affected by what white people thought of us. There was another thing, though, and that was being on the basketball, baseball, and track teams. I'm pretty sure I didn't think about it consciously, but I believe being a part of those teams made me feel better about myself in every way.

My reasons for wanting to go to college were mixed and probably rather fuzzy. My family was poor and the whole Cherokee community was poor, and I thought that if I went away and got an education, it might help all of us in some way. But there was another reason, a reason that involved my father. He was a remarkable man in many ways. He had very little formal education himself, but he understood its value.

He had had an unusual experience as a young man. He fought in World War I and had been in a battalion that had a number of Indians from Arizona, who were probably Navajos and Apaches but whom he just called desert Indians. They were the first Indians from that part of the country he had ever met, and he was deeply interested in them. He also learned that—as bad off as the Cherokees were in lots of ways—the desert Indians were much worse off, especially in the kind of education they were getting in those days. My father used to talk about them a lot, and he had a wish, what we Cherokees call a life wish, that some day one of his children would go out there and help them. Someplace along the way I got it in my mind that I might be the one. That meant going to college first.

I'll never forget the day I told the principal of the Centralia high school that I was going to college. I thought he might tell me some things about college and help me decide where to go. I remember I went to his office during lunchtime, and he was alone, sitting at his desk eating a sandwich.

I stood in the doorway and just blurted out, "I'm going to college."

He looked up and saw who it was standing there, and he broke out laughing, a real big belly laugh, and he got choked on his sandwich and started coughing. His face turned red, and I thought for a few seconds I should run for help, but then he got the bite down and started laughing again. He knew I was serious, but he couldn't believe it. He had to wipe tears out of his eyes.

"Now, Leroy," he said, when he could talk, "you just forget about going to college. You'll do well to get through high school. Then you can marry one of those pretty Cherokee girls and start raising papooses. That'll keep you busy."

I knew he wasn't going to give me any help about going to college, and I was mad, about as mad as I have ever been, I guess. It was just another case of an Indian being told he wasn't good for much, but this time it didn't make me feel bad or ashamed. It made me furious.

"I'll show you," I said, and I turned around and ran out of his office.

I told my father and mother I was going to college, and they didn't say I couldn't or shouldn't. My father was pleased. I could tell. I would be the first in the family to go.

Today, in 1983, just about all Indian boys and girls who finish high school in good standing can get scholarships to help them go to college. It wasn't that way when I went. My father and uncles pooled all the cash that they could spare, and it came to five dollars and eighty-five cents. That was my scholarship. It was enough to get me to within twenty miles of Oklahoma A. & M. College on the bus. I hitchhiked the rest of the way.

Now I'm going to skip over my college years and my years in World War II and the Korean War so I can talk about today's young Indians and, as I said, their parents. After World War II I finished college, not at Oklahoma A. & M. but at Warner Pacific College and at Anderson College in Indiana. It was at Anderson that I met the girl I married. Later I did more college work in education on the West Coast and in Arizona.

My father died in 1950 while I was still at Anderson, and I decided that I would carry out his dream that one of his children would work among the desert Indians. If anyone was going to do it, I was the one because I had a college education. The whole family supported me in the decision. It would have been better for the family if I had gone into work that paid more than teaching—especially teaching in Indian schools—but my mother and my brothers and sisters and I all decided that the life wish of the man who had held our family together should be honored. It was a family decision and it was the Cherokee way.

So I became a teacher and principal in schools on the Navajo Reservation in Arizona. All considered, I had a good life there. After a while the Navajo people accepted me, although in some ways I was always an outsider, of course. In a minute I'm going to talk about the not-so-happy side of Navajo

Part of the Navajo Reservation

life, so let me say something first about the good side because at its best it can be just as good and satisfying as any way of life I've ever seen.

To begin with, there is the Navajo country itself. The desert and mountains and sky all come together in a way that is just beautiful. It's a harsh beauty, but there's nothing else like it that I know of, and Navajos have a feeling for their land that is hard to find the equal of. I don't know how many times in the late afternoon I have watched a solitary Navajo horseman riding toward home and heard him singing a sunset song. The song would drift across the desert, and the whole scene was about as peaceful as anything you could imagine. Just try to picture a commuter from New York singing a song about the beauty of the sunset on his way home to Hoboken.

Navajo traditions are deep and rich. After I had worked among the people for a few years, I didn't feel out of place going to their squaw dances, which are fun gatherings, and to naming ceremonies and even healing ceremonies. A healing ceremony, given for some sick member of a family, can last for up to nine days and nights. Scores, even hundreds, of people may come for these ceremonies, and the family giving one is expected to feed everyone who comes. I have seen a family's entire sheep flock wiped out feeding guests. I know it's hard for a non-Indian to understand such a thing, but I think Indians of other tribes understand it. It is an ancient tradition to be generous to friends who visit you. It is expected of you, and you do it gladly.

The Navajos' goal of living in harmony with nature and the world around them is expressed in beautiful songs, chants, and rituals. This beauty finds its way into their everyday speech and even in the names they give to people. I had several Navajo names—some of them not so complimentary—but the one I liked best was given to me after I had been teaching and working as a principal in Navajo country for a number of years. That name means "He Whose Children Come Back to Him." I was given that name for two reasons. First, the children I had taught would return after they were grown, to see me and sometimes bring their problems, just as they did when they were students. Second, their own children came to my school to be students, just as the parents had been.

So I saw and learned many good things about Navajo life, and I got to know hundreds of Navajos who were good and loving parents to their children. But there was and still is a dark side to Navajo life rooted in their wretched poverty, and, of course, I came to know that too. Most Navajo men simply can't make a decent living for their families. The land is beautiful, but most of it is not suited to agriculture. The reservation is big

Perhaps this Navajo schoolboy senses that life will not be easy when he grows up.

but so is the Navajo tribe—the biggest in the United States—and there's not nearly enough grazing land for sheep and cattle. There is little industry, except mining coal and converting it to power. That gives jobs to some in the mining areas, but it's only a small number.

Most of the children who came to the schools where I taught and was principal were from very poor families, and many of them brought some terrible problems with them. In more cases than I like to think about, their fathers were alcoholics and sometimes their mothers, too. Sometimes in drunken rages their fathers beat them or their brothers and sisters and their mothers. Often they came out of homes where there wasn't enough to eat and no money for clothes. You add to those problems the fact that most of them spoke poor English, or none, when they started school, and you can see that it would be pretty hard for them to have a positive outlook on life or feel very good about themselves.

Sometimes it could be heartbreaking. I remember a boy telling me what a great dad he had, how many sheep and cattle he had, and bragging about how they would go hunting together. The next day I learned that the boy had never known his father, that he was a drunk who had deserted his family just after the boy was born. In time I came to learn that many Navajo youngsters invented fathers, and sometimes mothers, who no longer existed.

Another time I took a class to the town of Gallup on a field trip to learn some things about city government. One of our visits was to the jail. We just looked into the cell block, but, do you know, the mother of one of the students was sitting there in the drunk tank. Bad. Really bad. You can bet I never again included the jail on our city field trips.

Our constant task was to find ways to help these boys and girls build their confidence so that they could learn and succeed in school.

The ways I found to build confidence, to make them feel better about themselves, were no different from what would work anywhere else, I guess. Scouting was one. We always had Boy and Girl Scout troops in my schools. Being part of an organized activity was good, something special that they could have in common with other kids. Passing the Scout tests and working at getting merit badges was something they could handle, and every time they passed a test or got a merit badge, it was a little bit of success. There were Scout camps to go to, and somehow we always managed to find a way to send our troop.

Working on science projects was another thing. At first they would think they couldn't do anything. But a good teacher could show them that they could, and then we would have a science fair, and people would come in and admire their work. An annual science fair got to be a big thing, involving a number of schools. A good sports program was important, too. After my boyhood, no one had to tell me about that.

Of course, we didn't solve all the problems. We didn't solve half the problems, and they will never be solved until the problems of poverty on the reservations are solved. The fact is that western Indian tribes have never recovered from the original historical mistake and injustice of being confined to reservations made up of some of the poorest and most unproductive land in the United States.

The federal government has never been able to make up its mind about reservations and the Indians who live on them. Different administrations have flip-flopped between trying to make the reservations better places to live, on the one hand, and ending government support on the other.

Indians have been caught in the middle of that confusion. They have their cultures and they want to keep them, but they don't want to starve, so they leave the reservation or think about leaving. It really is that confusion, that sense of not knowing what to do, or whether they can do anything about what has happened to them, that causes the problems I have been talking about.

DR. FALLING and his wife, who is not an Indian, have three sons and a daughter, all of whom were raised on Indian reser-

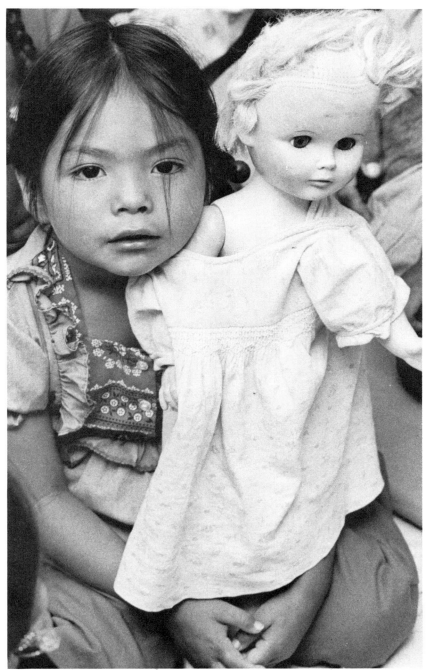

A Navajo schoolgirl with her doll

Stanton Falling, with his French horn

vations where Lee was teaching. One of the sons is now a computer engineer, another has gone into the ministry, and the third is working toward a career as a French horn player in a symphonic orchestra. The daughter is a data processor and is studying for a degree in education.

"I don't think they ever felt inferior because of their Indian blood," says Lee. "I don't think they had any more self-image problems than the average white child growing up. And I don't think any Indians would if they had reasonable economic security and the family support that accompanies that security.

Poor self-image isn't something that happens just because a person is an Indian."

Lee and his wife have left it up to their children to decide what part their Indian ancestry will play in their lives. The daughter and one of the sons have become enrolled members of the Cherokee tribe, but how much that will affect them in the future remains to be seen.

Stanton Falling, the French horn player, is not sure either what his Indianness means to him or what it may mean in the future. He does have a deep feeling for Native American music, a feeling he can trace in part to the songs and dances he heard and saw on the Navajo reservation and other nearby reservations, particularly the Hopi. Stanton took his master's degree in music at Washington State University, specializing in the French horn, and he also did research into the music of West Coast Indian tribes under a Music Department assistantship. He was a team teacher in a course on Native American music at the University.

"I don't believe I have that poor self-image problem we've been talking about," Stanton says with a smile. "There probably are less than three hundred jobs in the whole world for symphonic French horn players, and I intend to get one of them."

The chances are he will. He has already been a member of the Spokane Symphony Orchestra and played for seven months with orchestras in Germany. After some time back in the United States, he returned to Germany for more study and is now playing French horn in the Wiesbaden Opera orchestra.

▲▲▲▲▲▲▲▲▲▲▲▲▲▲▲▲▲▲▲

4

A New Vision of Indian Education

T HE HISTORY of education for American Indians is not a pretty story. From earliest times most Americans seemed to think that Indians should be "assimilated" into the white culture as quickly as possible. That point of view held that there was little of value in the Indians' way of life and that their religions and philosophies were those of uncivilized heathens. The few persons who argued otherwise were seldom listened to.

"The Indians must conform to the white man's ways, peaceably if they will, forcibly if they must," said Commissioner of Indian Affairs Thomas Morgan in 1889.

By the end of the nineteenth century most western Indian tribes had been confined to reservations. The buffalo were gone, farmers and ranchers had come, and the Indians could no longer range across the land that once had been theirs. It was easy for the "civilizing" agents of government to reach them.

An early U.S. government action to break down the fiber

of Indian tribes was the Religious Crimes Code. This code forbade Indians to hold their religious ceremonial dances, such as the Sun Dance, Corn Dance, and Rain Dance, and the feasts that were a part of ancient tribal rites. Medicine men were forbidden to perform their ceremonies or lead prayers. Even parents were forbidden to teach their children the customs, traditions, and legends of the tribe. Anyone who did these things could be put in jail. Most of the tribes secretly continued to practice their religions and teach their children tribal lore, but the Religious Crimes Code created terrible problems for tribal leaders.

It was through education, however, that assimilationists saw the major opportunity to pull young Indians away from their tribal cultures. A number of Christian churches were authorized by the Bureau of Indian Affairs to establish boarding schools for Indians. In time the Bureau also started its own boarding schools. These schools, both church-run and Bureau-run, were frequently far away from the reservations, and Indian children who had never been away from their families and tribes were forced to attend them.

Often loving Indian parents tried to hide their children from Bureau authorities. Sometimes parents were sent to jail for their actions, and no one listened when they tried to explain that their children had always gone to school, that school for them was learning to live in the world of nature around them. Their teachers were their parents and the elders of the tribe. Many times Indian children ran away from the boarding schools and somehow made their way back to their tribe. But government officers came to take them back again.

Many Indians of older generations have described their experiences attending boarding schools. The recollections of John Woodenlegs of the Northern Cheyenne tribe are typical. "The teachers wanted to make us into white children," Mr.

A graduate of a BIA high school in Oklahoma

Woodenlegs said. "They wouldn't let us talk about our homes or play Indian games or wear Indian clothes. We were taught that everything Indian was bad. If we said even one word of Cheyenne or any other Indian language, we were slapped or had our ears pulled. We didn't know any English, but that was the only language used in the schools. If we didn't do every-thing we were told to do, we were punished. Well, I learned English, but I always thought there should have been a better way to run those schools."

An old Comanche Indian from Oklahoma recalled being punished in school for speaking in the Comanche language. The teacher would make him hold a rubber band in his teeth and snap it against his lips. "But they couldn't keep us from whispering in Comanche in the dormitory at night," he said, "and they couldn't keep us from remembering our homes. When we went to bed and the lights were out, in our thoughts and our dreams we were Indians."

It was not until the administration of President Franklin D. Roosevelt in 1934 that the U.S. government made a major change in its policy regarding Indians. In that year the Indian Reorganization Act was passed by the U.S. Congress and a number of reforms in the treatment of Indians became law. Among the most important, Indian tribes were given freedom to practice their traditional religions and to preserve and restore their native cultures.

But the injustices of decades cannot be erased overnight, and while there were improvements from the 1930s, it was not until the great civil rights movements of the mid-1960s and early 1970s that dramatic changes in the education of young Indians began to take place, and they came about through the efforts of the Indians themselves. The Navajos, by far the largest American Indian tribe with more than 175,000 members, were leaders in those changes.

THE NAVAJO ACADEMY in Farmington, New Mexico, was born out of a dream. Educational leaders of the tribe had long envisioned a school on or near the Navajo Reservation where gifted and highly motivated young Navajo men and women could receive a top quality college preparatory education. The school would have the very highest standards in its English, mathematics, science, and social studies programs.

But it would have something else. A part of the core curriculum would be study of Navajo language, Navajo history, Navajo philosophy and traditions, Navajo fine arts. The gradu-

Students at the Navajo Academy in Farmington, New Mexico

ates of this school would be fully prepared to undertake college and university study. But they would take from the school an understanding and appreciation of their Navajo heritage. They would be prepared to function effectively in a rapidly changing world, both Navajo and non-Navajo.

That was the dream, and it came into being in 1977 when the Navajo Academy was created with full tribal backing and special funds available for Indian education. Word of the new school went out across the reservation and applications were invited. But it was made very clear that graduation requirements would exceed state requirements in almost every category. The Academy would require three times more math and science than the state, for example. Anyone who thought these requirements were too demanding was not encouraged to apply for admission.

The challenge was accepted, and today, seven years after it opened its doors, the Navajo Academy is a thriving institution. It is small, with an enrollment planned not to go above 175, but it is expected to produce leaders of the tribe.

"We can't be sure they will return to the reservation after they have finished their college education," says one senior Navajo official, "but we believe that many will. We think the program at the Academy will help with that."

The specific part of the program he was referring to is that dealing with Navajo culture, history, language, and contemporary affairs such as the present and future economic development of the reservation. Almost without exception the students have entered into this part of their education with enthusiasm.

"I couldn't speak my own language when I came here," says one student. "Can you imagine that? I thought I would be the only one in the school like that, but I wasn't, not by a long shot. But we're learning now and it feels good to be able to say things in Navajo."

"Do you know how the courses in Navajo history and culture made me feel at first?" asks one girl. "Ashamed. Ashamed that I knew so little about myself and my people. And then I got mad. Why didn't I know anything? Why hadn't I been taught? Now I'm not ashamed or mad. I'm just glad I'm finding out who I am."

Ernesteen Lynch is a teacher of Navajo history at the Academy, and she does not find it at all surprising that most of her students know so little about the subject when they first come to her class. "I'm a Navajo," she says, "but I grew up not knowing anything about Navajo history, culture, or philosophy. My parents were Christians, and they were negative about Navajo ways. They were like so many of their generation

Ernesteen Lynch, teacher at the Navajo Academy

who believed that the way to get along in life was to try not to be an Indian."

Ernesteen believes that the BIA schools and most Christian churches on the reservation, at least in the past, tried to make Navajos forget their culture. "Some churches even put pressure on their members to burn their corn pollen bags," she says. "Pollen bags are sacred to Navajos. They are symbols of purity and the eternal. And, of course, you've heard about how schools punished children for speaking Indian languages. And those are just some of the things that were done, just a few."

Ernesteen believes that the conflicts brought about in the Navajo mind by acts such as these have resulted in serious damage to a great many Navajos. And she believes that the same is true for other tribes. She thinks the results have been confusion and a poor self-image that have led to many adjustment problems.

Ernesteen studied history in college and after she graduated she returned to teach in a junior high school on the Navajo Reservation. She had not learned any Navajo history or culture in college, but she had learned how to do research. As a teacher of history, it just did not seem right to her that she did not know her own history.

The result was that she built a course in Navajo history and culture and received permission to teach it. "The children were fascinated," she says, "and I know it reached some of them deep down. Occasionally I run into an old student who still mentions that course. There was a boy back from Vietnam who told me that, crawling through the fields over there, some of the things we had talked about came into his mind and made the bad times easier to get through."

Students at the Navajo Academy take four years of both English and Navajo language, with the Navajo program adjusted according to the students' knowledge of the language

A music lesson at the Navajo Academy

when they enter the school. And in addition to standard social studies courses such as American history, world history, geography, and civics, the Navajo Academy students study tribal government, American Indian history, and Navajo history, culture, philosophy, and arts.

Dillon Platero, a Navajo, was the prime mover in the Navajo Academy's establishment and is its present headmaster. "We are creating a school in which the students are getting the best of both worlds," he says, "the best of Western culture and a far better knowledge of their own Navajo culture than they ever had before.

"We haven't had time to have much experience with grad-

A student at Farmington, New Mexico

uates," he adds, "but what we have had is promising. Out of eighteen Academy graduates who have entered college, fifteen are still there in their second year. That's at least a hundred percent better than the national average for Indians staying in college."

Although the Navajo Academy, with its demanding academic standards and complete bicultural approach, is the first Indian school of its kind in the country, it was not the first Navajo school to teach students about their history and culture. That distinction goes to a school started in 1966 in Rough Rock, a small community deep inside the reservation.

The director of the school, which became known as the

The playground at Rough Rock Demonstration School, one of the best schools on the Reservation.

Rough Rock Demonstration School, was Dr. Robert A. Roessel, an Anglo, as whites are often called in the Southwest. He had spent years teaching on the reservation, and his doctor's dissertation was based on visits he had made to over one hundred Navajo communities to talk with tribal elders about what kind of schooling they thought their children needed. It was this research that Roessel and a group of Navajo education leaders used to persuade the Bureau of Indian Affairs to budget money for the Rough Rock Demonstration School.

In the Demonstration School no opportunities were missed to help the children understand themselves as Navajos. Navajo decorations were freely mixed in with other classroom decorations. The library had a Navajo corner. Recordings of

A Navajo youngster with a party hat. He goes to the Rough Rock Demonstration School.

Navajo music were played at certain times during the school day. In the evenings old men, the historians and medicine men of the tribe, came to the dormitories and told Navajo folktales and legends. Biographies of successful Navajos were prepared by the school staff and used as part of the classroom teaching materials.

Thirty-five minutes of class time were set aside each day in the lower three grades and forty-five minutes in grades three through six during which the students would learn more about Navajo culture. Some of the first lessons covered the Navajo hogan: its history, how it is built, the ceremonies that surround it, and how life is conducted in it. Other lessons were about the best ways of farming and caring for livestock on the reservation. Still others dealt with Navajo history and how the tribal government works. Such subjects had never been covered before as a part of the regular school program.

Today, after more than fifteen years, the Rough Rock Demonstration School is still functioning, and the ideas tested there are going out to other schools on the reservation. Although Robert Roessel is no longer at the school, his philosophy is. He once summed up his feelings about education for Indians in this way: "Back when I was teaching on the reservation, I used to give my students a simple illustration. I told them they had two legs. One of them was their Navajo heritage, and the other was the best part of the white world. I told them they couldn't get along with just one leg but needed both to be secure and whole."

▲▲▲▲▲▲▲▲▲▲▲▲▲▲▲▲▲▲▲▲▲

5

Pictures on a Rock

O NE SPRING DAY a few years before the Rough Rock
Demonstration School was opened, a five-year-old
Navajo boy named Fred Bia was watching the family
sheep flock in the arid countryside near the little town. It was
his daily chore to follow the sheep as they drifted over the red,
rocky earth in their endless search for grass and the leaves of
semidesert plants. He had covered this ground so many times
that he no longer paid any attention to where he was, his
thoughts wandering as he moved slowly with the animals.

When he saw the rock in front of him, he knew he was in a
place that he had not been before, and he could not believe his
eyes. The big red rock was covered with drawings of people
and animals. Fred stood very still as he stared at them, and an
excitement he had never felt before raced through his blood.
Who had made these pictures? When? He had no idea. There
were no drawings on the other rocks around him, only those
he was staring at. He was almost hypnotized and though he
had no way of knowing it, in that moment Fred Bia, Navajo
artist, was born.

When he finally looked away from the rock, he saw that his sheep were nearly out of sight, and he ran to catch up with them. But he did not forget the drawings on the rock. He thought about them that night, and the next day he returned to the rock. The same feeling of excitement came back to him. He picked up a small chalky stone, went to a large rock nearby, and did his best to copy the drawings of people and animals he saw on the red rock.

Later that day in another part of the rocky semidesert where he had followed his sheep, Fred drew the pictures from memory on other rocks. In the days and weeks that followed he drew other pictures, some from his imagination, some from the things in nature around him. By the time he entered first grade, Fred's pictures covered many of the big rocks around Rough Rock.

In school Fred discovered crayons, and fortunately he had teachers who quickly saw that the boy had a real drawing ability and an unusual fascination with making pictures. They encouraged him and saw that he had plenty of crayons and paper. When Fred went to high school in Chinle and Fort Wingate the encouragement continued, and his powers as a pictorial artist grew.

After he graduated from high school, he was accepted as a student at the Institute of American Indian Art in Santa Fe. Fred began in elementary classes, but his instructors at this special school for promising Indian artists moved him to advanced classes.

Fred spent two years at the art institute and then embarked on a career as a professional artist. Today he is one of a small number of Indian artists whose work sells steadily and brings substantial prices. Major fame remains in the future, but he has established himself as a solid professional painter whose work is in a number of western art galleries and museums and

Navajo artist Fred Bia and his infant daughter

in such private collections as that of famous country-music singer Johnny Cash.

"I want to be thought of as a painter, not as a Navajo painter or an Indian painter," Fred says. "But I draw my subjects from the Navajo world, the people and the land, because that is what I know."

Fred returned to Rough Rock to live, and for the past three years he has given much of his time to illustrating a series of Navajo social studies books that the Rough Rock Demonstration School is producing for grades kindergarten through twelve. The books will be made available to all Navajo schools. His powerful black-and-white drawings of Black Mesa, Shiprock, and other Navajo landmarks, as well as faithful visual portraits of Navajo people and cultural objects, will give Navajo schoolchildren a new and exciting look at themselves and their world as Navajos.

Fred sometimes talks about the day that changed his life, the day he saw the drawings on the rock in the desert. He never learned how the drawings got there or what they were. He does not think they were ancient pictographs, although there are many of them in Navajo country. They may have been the work of a shaman or medicine man, but Fred does not think they were that either.

"They were just there, and I saw them," he says. "I am very glad I did."

▲▲▲▲▲▲▲▲▲▲▲▲▲▲▲▲▲▲▲▲

6

In the Shadow of the Sacred Mesa

THE 640-square-mile Zuni Reservation in western New Mexico is in isolated country, a land of sagebrush, cedar, piñon, and rocky escarpments encircling a plain where sheep and cattle graze. Their geographical isolation, coupled with a language isolation—strangely the Zuni language is unrelated to any other Indian language—has enabled the Zuni tribe to keep much of its traditional culture intact.

The pueblo dwellings in the old part of the town of Zuni are similar to those that the Spanish conquistadores saw when they first entered the country in 1540. The "beehive" ovens used by Zuni women for baking bread and roasting green corn are timeless. Many Zunis of the older generation speak no language except their tribal tongue.

Most Zunis are Catholics, a legacy of the Spanish conquest, and the seventeenth-century mission church of Our Lady of Guadalupe is the largest and most impressive building in Zuni. But like so many other American Indian tribes, the Zunis' traditional tribal religion has remained very important to them.

The Zuni religion is presided over by sacred societies such as the Bow Priesthood, and religion is an integral part of all activities of the Zuni people. The religion is complex and filled with ceremony and ritual. On many afternoons and nights a visitor to Zuni will hear drums beating and see dancers in masks and religious regalia. The Zuni Shalako ceremonial dances and blessing of new houses are most important, and every year hundreds of Zunis who have left the mother pueblo return for the great event. There are many Zuni spirits called Kachinas, but at the heart of the tribe's religion is the belief that man must live in harmony with the world of nature around him.

It might seem that the traditional world of the Zunis is so powerful and ever-present that it would be impossible for the modern world to intrude into this ancient pueblo culture. That is not the case.

SHORTLY AFTER taking office as Governor of the Zuni tribe in 1966, Robert Lewis had carried out a house-to-house survey of practically the whole Zuni population. He wanted to find out what they thought would make a better life for the Zuni people. The range of answers that poured in was truly astonishing. The desire for jobs that would pay a decent wage came first by a large margin. Improved quality of sheep and cattle was often mentioned, as was better housing. But beyond these basics, the Zuni people made known their desire for the kinds of things that most American towns take for granted.

They wanted paved streets, streetlights, a hospital, better phones, an improved sewer system, a public library. And they wanted other things: a supermarket, swimming pool, trash barrels, movie theater, Little League baseball, root beer stand. And those were only a small part of the final list. It was made abundantly clear to Governor Lewis and the Tribal Council that, while Zunis place great value on their customs and traditions, most of the people of the tribe want a share of modern American culture.

As one young Zuni man put it, "I don't think that improving the quality of life on the reservation means that we have to lose our culture. If we don't make life better on reservations, how can we expect people to stay on them, especially young people?"

A dynamic, hard-working man, Governor Lewis was successful in getting major government support for economic development of the Zuni Reservation. But he wanted something equally important: He wanted the development and changes to be brought about by the Zuni people and not by outsiders who would be brought in to do the work for them. Again Lewis was successful, this time in convincing Washington to let the Zuni tribe try a new experiment in self-determination and self-reliance. The plan called for almost all Bureau of Indian Affairs programs providing services to the Zuni tribe to be controlled and operated by Zuni tribal employees. The money to be made available for development on the reservation would be handled by the tribal government and not by the BIA.

In the years since that first survey, much has been accomplished. Over 470 new low-cost housing units have been built. A forty-five bed, comprehensive community health hospital has been completed and is in operation. Grazing lands for sheep and cattle have been improved. Over eleven miles of village streets have been paved. New bridges have been constructed. A local radio station is now on the air. New schools are being built. Plans for a museum of Zuni history and culture have been started, and a great many other projects have been completed or are under way.

There have been problems and many can be traced to the

Calbert Seciwa, a young Zuni leader. In the background is the sacred mesa, Dowa Yalanne.

fact that not enough trained and experienced Zunis are available to carry out the ambitious development program. Slowly, however, that problem is being overcome as young Zunis are going out to receive training and then returning to the reservation.

Such a person is Calbert A. Seciwa—"Cal" to his friends and associates—who for several years has been Director of the Zuni Economic Development Program. Cal is a Zuni who, in fact, spent little time on the reservation while he was growing up. His parents worked in the nearby towns of Gallup and Fort Wingate, and Cal went to school in Gallup. After high school he took a degree at Fort Lewis College in Colorado and then returned to Zuni to be a teacher.

One of the biggest problems that the Zuni tribe had to overcome was the dropout rate of Zuni secondary school students, which was one of the highest in the state of New Mexico. The problem, as Cal and other concerned leaders saw it, was primarily a confusion caused by the fast pace of development set side by side with the age-old traditions and culture of the Zuni tribe.

In order to help solve that problem the Zuni tribe established an Alternative Learning Center for students who would not or could not attend the regular high school on the reservation. Cal taught social studies for four years at this very special school.

The building chosen for the school was a Shalako house, a building where one of the most important Zuni sacred ceremonies was once held. The curriculum of the school was one that gave the students the necessary math, English, and other courses needed for a high school diploma, but there were also courses and special activities that dealt with the relevance of Zuni culture in the present-day world.

The Alternative Learning Center has had unusual success in helping students to graduation. When the public school system came under Zuni community control in 1980, the Learning Center was made a part of the Zuni Public School District.

It was during his years of teaching at the Learning Center that Cal began to look at other areas of need of the Zuni people. What he saw made him decide to return to school, and he became a student at the American Indian Law Center at the University of New Mexico. There Cal received special instruction in Indian law and in United States government programs for American Indians. As a part of his training Cal spent several months as an intern at the Office of Management and Budget in Washington, D.C., and it was that experience that made him decide he was ready to return to the Zuni Reservation and

Zuni students

become a part of the development program there. Quickly he established himself as a valuable member of the development team responsible, among other things, for the Comprehensive Development Plan so necessary to securing government project funds.

Sometimes when visitors come to see the Zuni Economic Development Program, Cal will take them first to a plain some distance from the village of Zuni and stop almost in the shadow of the sacred mesa called Dowa Yalanne, which means "Corn Mountain."

"In our legends," he will tell his visitors, "the Zuni people were guided to this place by a giant water spider during ancient times. His eight legs stretched out in all directions, and as far as they reached was Zuni land. The center of the world was the spot covered by the spider's heart, and the Zuni people built their pueblos surrounding that spot.

"Our legends tell of a great flood," Cal continues. "To escape the flooding waters the ancient Zuni people climbed to the top of Dowa Yalanne, but the water kept rising and was about to wash over the top of the mesa. It was decided by the religious leaders of the tribe that one of the priests should sacrifice his two children to the gods, who were surely angry at something the Zuni people had done. The priest made the sacrifice and immediately the rains stopped. When the waters receded, the priest's two children could be seen carved in stone by the ebb and flow of the water."

Cal will turn and point. There on an edge of the mesa can be seen two forms side by side, shaped by nature in the red sandstone. In the bright New Mexico sun their resemblance to two human beings requires little imagination. "That is why the beautiful mesa is sacred to the Zuni," Cal tells his visitors. "It is the place that has always served as a sanctuary for the Zuni people. In historic times the people retreated once again to the top of the mesa when raids of enemy tribes became too bad, and they lived there during the Great Pueblo Revolt of 1680 against the Spaniards.

"There are many legends and events in my people's history which have taught them valuable lessons for conducting their lives," Cal concludes. "One of the most important of these lessons—one a Zuni must never forget—is that one must never place anything above the well-being of the entire tribe."

And then Cal will begin the tour of economic development projects in Zuni.

▲▲▲▲▲▲▲▲▲▲▲▲▲▲▲▲▲▲▲

7

Between Two Worlds

W HILE the afternoon sun was still high, Jason, the fire keeper, went to the place of the sweat lodge, which was large enough to hold many men. He put pumice stones in the fire pit opposite the lodge, heaped wood on top of them, and used sweet grass to start a blaze. Soon the fire was roaring.

As he worked, Jason tried not to look at the prison walls around him. He tried to imagine that this was a sweat lodge on his reservation in New Mexico. But it was hard to pretend when he could see the correctional officer watching him from the gun tower and when he saw the other Indian prisoners, almost twenty of them in their gray-green prison clothes, walking toward the sweat lodge to take part in the ancient purification ceremony.

The pumice stones had grown fiery hot and, using a bucket scoop, Jason carried them into the sweat lodge. He put them in a pit in the center and sprinkled in sacred herbs as the medicine man had taught him. Then Jason and the other Indian prisoners removed their clothes and sat in a circle around the pit. The water pourer rose and poured a bucket of cold water on the pumice stones, and instantly the lodge was filled with hot steam. It was then that Jason called out the ritual invitation to his tribal spirits to join in the sweat bath, while Indians from other tribes did the same.

Now the medicine man entered the tepee and joined the circle. He was a Cheyenne who lived near the prison, and he had come many times to teach the proper way to have a sweat bath and to lead the prayers and singing. Although Jason was not a Cheyenne, he had learned the Cheyenne songs, and they reminded him of those he had heard on his reservation. The songs asked the spirit powers to give peace to the men who took part in the ceremony and to look kindly on them.

More water was poured on the pumice stones, which held heat for a long time, and steam continued to billow up. It grew very hot inside the lodge, and sweat poured from Jason's body and face. The voice of the medicine man rose in a rhythmic, hypnotic chant, and sometimes Jason and the other men joined in the songs. He lost track of time as the heat and the songs washed over him. He felt that he was some place where there were no walls, and he was happy.

When the stones began to cool and the singing, prayers, and ritual bath were finished, Jason and the other prisoners returned to their cell blocks. Jason always felt cleaner after the ritual washing than he did when he took a shower in the prison. After dinner, Jason went directly to his cell, which he shared with two other men, neither of them Indians. He went quickly to bed, as he always did after visiting the sweat lodge. There was a time when his cellmates had made jokes about his taking part in the sweat lodge purification ceremony, but they no longer did that.

Usually Jason went to sleep easily after he had been in the

Jason, an Indian prisoner at El Reno, Oklahoma

sweat lodge, but tonight there was something to think about that kept him wide awake. That morning he had learned of the parole board's decision to transfer him to a halfway house in Albuquerque. He would get help in finding a job, and he could go out during the day but must spend nights in the halfway house. After three months, if he did well, he would be paroled. He would be free again.

What would he do then? It seemed to Jason that he had thought of little else during the two years he had been in prison. But now that the time of his release was near and not some vague possibility in the future, he was not certain. He would return to the reservation to see his mother and sister. He was sure of that. Now that he had a high school diploma, he might go to college. Before he was sent to prison, the thought of college had never occurred to him. He had become interested in computers in prison, and he thought he might go to a computer school in Albuquerque or maybe Phoenix.

Jason had talked to Father Bob, the prison chaplain, many times about these things, and there would be time to talk some more before he was transferred to the halfway house later in the month. He was glad of that.

Many Indian prisoners at the Federal Correctional Institution at El Reno, Oklahoma, have had reason to be glad that the Reverend Robert C. Allanach, O.M.I., is there. As chaplain, Father Bob, as he is known to inmates and prison staff alike, is responsible for offering pastoral care to all prisoners. But during his years at this federal prison, he has developed a special concern for American Indians, who have higher arrest and conviction rates—mainly for drinking-related offenses—than any other racial group in the country.

Father Bob's concern stems in part at least from the fact that his religious order is Oblates of Mary Immaculate, whose traditional mission has been to help disadvantaged and oppressed people—the abandoned of the earth, as Father Bob puts it. He places American Indians squarely in that category.

"They are the most depressed people as a race that I have ever worked with," he says. "They have been told for hundreds of years that they are no damned good. They have had their land taken away, their religion taken away, their language taken away, their pride taken away." And, he adds flatly, "They have been kicked around ever since the white race came to this continent.

"They are lonely," Father Bob continues, speaking of the Indian prisoners he has known. "It is hard for them to express themselves toward others, to make gestures of friendship, to seek companionship."

Father Bob thinks the reason for this probably is rooted in the low esteem in which many Indians—especially those who have suffered the additional defeat of being sent to prison—hold themselves. They are afraid of rejection if they reach out to others. Although Indians make up less than 1 percent of the American population, the number of Indian prisoners in the El Reno institution averages about 5 percent of the inmate total. The reason for this is that they lived on or near reservations under federal jurisdiction and therefore were sent to a federal prison rather than a state institution. At any given time Father Bob may be concerned with fifty to sixty Indian prisoners, most of them young.

"Almost all of them are school dropouts," says Father Bob. "They have been convicted of a crime using force or they wouldn't be in this particular prison. Most of them were into heavy drinking or drugs or both when they were arrested. How can you help young men like these develop some positive feelings about themselves? What does it take to get a little pride growing there?"

There are no easy answers to those questions, but the best

Father Bob and a young Indian inmate at the federal prison in El Reno

ones Father Bob has found are basically those that have guided his work with troubled young people in other assignments. "You listen to them," he says. "You show them some respect and, yes, some love."

From listening, Father Bob learned that the sweat lodge ceremony with its purification and cleansing symbolism was an integral part of some of the Indian prisoners' religion. They asked the chaplain if there wasn't some way this part of their religious observance could be carried out. Father Bob, sensing the sincerity of the request, went to the warden and received approval to have the sweat lodge built on the prison grounds on a trial basis. He arranged for the lodge, for the heat-holding pumice stones, and for a medicine man to conduct the ceremony. The sweat lodge has now become a significant part of prison life for many of the Indian inmates.

A number of the Indian prisoners carry medicine bags containing sacred pollen and other sacred materials of their tribal religion. Sometimes the bags must be inspected, and when that is the case, Father Bob is always called in to examine them. Because the bags contain sacred materials, the Indian inmates have an agreement with the warden that no one on the prison staff except Father Bob will open them for inspection. They know that he understands their meaning and importance.

Many of the Indian inmates know very little about the history and culture of their tribes. Father Bob encourages them to learn as much as they can about their tribal roots. He does this through weekly discussion groups in which Indian prisoners who are more knowledgeable about traditions of their tribe talk with the others and answer questions. He also brings in specialists in Indian history and culture and arranges the showing of cultural films about Indians.

"Indians have a culture and history to be proud of," says Father Bob. "The more they realize that, the more likely they are to see themselves in a better light."

BEFORE HE LEFT for the halfway house, Jason talked about how he came to be in the El Reno prison and about his experiences there. "I was caught between two worlds," he said. "I never knew where I wanted to be or where I was supposed to be—on the reservation where I was born and grew up or in town where I went to high school.

"Don't get me wrong. I'm not making excuses. I'm in this prison because I did stupid things. But it's true that I kept drifting back and forth between the reservation where there was nothing to do and the town where I didn't feel like I belonged and didn't know what to do. By the eleventh grade I was drinking a lot, smoking marijuana, and hanging out with a gang of school dropouts. They did things like breaking into cars to get things to sell, and I did some of that too.

"Then the gang planned to rip off a service station. I was with them when they talked about it, but I decided that wasn't for me. They got caught. Nobody was hurt, but they had used a gun and that made it serious. I was taken in with the others and convicted of concealing the knowledge of a felony.

"I'll never forget being brought to this place, handcuffed. I felt like an animal that had been caught in a trap. I was scared and mad and I couldn't do a thing about it. I got into the prison routine, and it was like being in a cage. At night when I was in my bunk trying to go to sleep, my mind would go back to when I was a boy, maybe five or six years old, tending sheep. The country was big and flat and there were blue mountains in the distance. That was the way I thought about being free, just walking out there, following sheep.

"I met some of the other Indians in the prison and that helped a little. I had never gone to a sweat lodge on the reservation, but I started going here, mainly just because it was something to do. But I found that I really liked it, and I haven't missed a time since I started. I had seen Father Bob and heard about him, but I didn't have a real talk with him for maybe a couple of months. He doesn't push himself on a new prisoner, but you know he's there if you want to see him.

"I did go to talk with him after a while. He didn't try to preach or lay any heavy talk on me, but after I had seen him a couple of times, I decided to get my high school diploma through the study program that the prison had. And I started going to the Indian history discussion groups that he had at night.

"My mother wanted to come from the reservation to visit me. I wasn't sure it was a good idea, but Father Bob thought it was. I was working in the prison broom factory and making a little money. After about a year I had saved enough to buy bus tickets for her and my sister to come to El Reno. Father Bob found them a place to stay and helped them get to the prison. It was great to see them, but it was hard, too, really hard. They both cried when they saw me, and none of us could say very much at first. But their visit did something for me. It made me swear to myself that I would never cause them that kind of trouble and shame again in my life. I don't think I will.

"The time in this place hasn't been all wasted. I have my high school diploma, and I've learned some things about myself and about being an Indian. I'm glad Father Bob was here."

ONE OF the last things Jason did before leaving for the halfway house was take part in the powwow that Father Bob arranges every year for the Indian prisoners. The chaplain goes to his many friends for help, including getting a deer for roasting. He sees that the berry sauce, wild rice, fry bread, and other foods of a traditional powwow are in abundance. Indians from the community come in for the dancing and the giveaway, a centuries-old Indian practice of gift sharing.

"I'm not trying to save souls," Father Bob says, "and I don't think other chaplains are. We are trying to make the prisoner's day a little better, a little more worthwhile. That may make a difference later on."

8

Los Indios

T HE Vanishing American has stubbornly refused to vanish. Time after time tribes that were thought to have ceased to exist or to be on the brink of extinction have proved how tough the fiber of the American Indian really is. Probably no better example of this toughness of spirit, this determination to survive, can be found than the tiny Tigua tribe of Texas. The Tigua story is one of how age and youth combined to bring about a near-miracle of survival.

TIGUA HISTORY reaches back a long way in the history of the American Southwest. They were originally a part of the Tiwa Pueblo Indian tribe of New Mexico, and as such their culture can be traced back as far as 1500 B.C. The Tiwa, together with such other pueblos as Taos, Zuni, Hopi, and San Ildefonso, were highly developed agricultural communities when, in 1540, Coronado led the first Spanish troops into what is now New Mexico.

The Pueblo Indians came under Spanish control, and many of them were converted to Christianity. Finally, however, the harsh Spanish rule became intolerable, and in 1680 the pueblos revolted. Although they later returned in greater force, the Spaniards were forced to retreat into Mexico, and a group of Tiwa Pueblo Indians went with them. History does not make clear whether the Spaniards forced this band of Tiwas to accompany them or whether they went voluntarily because they had become Christians.

In any case, in 1681 they established a new pueblo near the mountain pass called El Paso del Norte, and in 1682 they built a mission church there in honor of Saint Anthony, their patron saint. They became known as the Tiguas of Ysleta del Sur—the Tiwas of Isleta of the South. Tigua is the Spanish spelling of Tiwa and the pronunciation (tee-wa) is the same.

For a long time the Tiguas lived happily on the banks of the Rio Grande, raising corn, beans, chiles, and other crops and hunting in the nearby Hueco Mountains. Their life in every important way was the same as it had been in the mother pueblo to the north.

In 1751 King Charles V of Spain made a formal land grant to the Tigua Indians of Ysleta del Sur. The king already had made similar grants to the Indian pueblos of New Mexico. The Tiguas' grant gave them title to a thirty-six-square-mile area surrounding their mission. With that grant the Tigua's future seemed assured.

But major political and social changes were on the horizon. In 1821 Mexico gained its independence from Spain, and in 1827 Juan Maria Ponce de Leon established a settlement just a few miles from the Tigua pueblo that over time grew into the city of El Paso. During those years settlers from the United States were moving into the Southwest in increasing numbers, and in 1836 Texas declared its independence from Mexico.

After a decade as a republic, Texas joined the United States as the twenty-eighth state. From 1846 to 1848 the Mexican-American War was fought.

In 1863, under the administration of Abraham Lincoln, the United States government officially agreed that all of the southwestern pueblos—with one exception—owned the land that they had received under the Spanish grants. The exception was the Tigua pueblo. The failure of the United States to recognize the Tiguas' right to their land probably resulted from the fact that Texas had seceded from the Union in 1861, and the Tiguas—through none of their own doing—were a part of the Confederacy when the pueblos in New Mexico and Arizona received their land patents.

Even after the Civil War the federal government failed to recognize the Tiguas' land title, and in 1871 the tribe was dealt a crippling blow when the Texas State Legislature passed a law making the Tigua pueblo a part of the city of Ysleta and giving the city government the right to dispose of the Indians' land to settlers.

The law was later declared unconstitutional, but the damage had been done. The Tiguas were quickly dispossessed of their land by illegal means. Almost overnight their traditional way of life was destroyed, and they became a small group of urban dwellers surrounded by a sea of Anglos and Mexican-Americans that poured into the attractive El Paso area.

No longer able to make a living by farming and hunting, unskilled and untrained for urban work, the Tiguas sank to the lowest rung of the economic ladder. Unemployment among them was well over 50 percent. Alcoholism was common. In the midst of English and Spanish speakers, they found their Tiwa language slipping away. Marriage outside the tribe also took its toll on language and tribal customs. The Tiguas sent their children to school, but so poor was the morale of both parents and children that the dropout rate by the sixth grade ranged as high as 90 percent.

By the mid-1960s almost every Tigua house was in danger of being lost through nonpayment of taxes; and, although most people in the El Paso area knew that a group of Indians lived in the suburb of Ysleta, the general belief was that they no longer existed as a tribe. Mexican-Americans who lived nearby called them simply "los indios"—the Indians. So far as they were concerned, these Indians did not even have a tribal name. Anthropologists who looked into the matter agreed that the Tigua tribe was dead.

But this time they and everyone else were wrong. Most Tiguas lived close together in a run-down section of Ysleta, and they kept very much to themselves. What the general public did not know was that the Tiguas had never ceased to have their own tribal government consisting of a traditional leader called Cacique, always the oldest man in the tribe, plus an elected governor and council. It was the same form of government that the Tigua and all other pueblos had had since long before the coming of the Spaniards; and though the Tigua government now was almost without power, it still served to remind the Tigua people that they were a special group.

And while poverty and urban life had weakened the tribe, the Tiguas, in their small housing area, had continued to practice many of their pueblo customs, to hold the ancient ceremonial dances, to eat the special foods. Nor had they ever ceased to go to the Hueco Mountains to find the herbs and plants the tribe had always used for medicine.

There was another thing, and it proved to be the most important. Existing in the minds of the tribal elders was an unwritten history of the Tigua people, a memory of all that they had done and been and of the ill fortunes that had befallen them. They believed that if the story of the Tigua could be properly put before the Texas government, they might receive some help in improving their lives.

The Tigua elders found the help they needed in an El Paso lawyer named Tom Diamond, a man with a sense of history and justice who agreed to assist the tribe in its efforts to gain legal recognition and to establish its land claims. Thus began a lengthy search through historical documents and legal records to establish their tribal roots and their centuries of functioning as a tribe, to prove that they had a legal claim to land that was taken from them.

The effort was successful. In 1967 the Texas State Legislature officially recognized the Tiguas as a Texas Indian tribe. The following year President Lyndon Johnson signed a federal bill which recognized the Tiguas as an American Indian tribe.

The Texas legislature created a small reservation of about twenty-eight acres for the Tiguas in the area of their original mission, which was still standing and still in use. In addition, the state set aside an area of ten thousand acres in the Hueco Mountains Wilderness and Wildlife Refuge—the Tiguas' ancestral hunting grounds—where the tribe can hunt and fish and collect herbs and plants for the making of traditional medicines. Most important, as a recognized Indian tribe, the Tiguas were now eligible to receive federal funds to help them in educational and other development programs.

The Tiguas had won a great victory, but it was only a beginning on the long road to a new life for the tribe. A housing program had to be started. Plans for producing tribal income had to be developed. Buildings for administration and social and business activities had to be built. Loans from the U.S. Department of Housing and Urban Development were secured for the housing and building program.

But the long-range future of the tribe lay in the development of its children and its young men and women. On that

Ray Apodaca

there was general agreement as well as concern. In the mid-1970s the school dropout rate of Tigua children by the time they reached the sixth grade was still around 90 percent. According to tribal estimates, the average level of schooling achieved by Tiguas was about the fourth grade.

In 1977 the Texas Indian Commission appointed Raymond D. Apodaca to be the Superintendent of the Tigua tribe. Under the Commission system the superintendent is the chief executive officer of the tribe and also the Commission's representative to the tribe. He works closely with the Governor and Tribal Council in carrying out all development programs.

In this case the appointment was particularly appropriate because Ray Apodaca is himself a Tigua Indian, one of the few young members of the tribe to achieve a college education. Ray attended New Mexico State University at Las Cruces, less than a hundred miles distant from Ysleta del Sur Pueblo, and when the offer came to be superintendent, he did not hesitate in accepting. Ray had earned a bachelor's degree in government and a master's degree in public administration, an academic background that could hardly have been better for his new job.

Working side by side with the tribe's elected officials, Ray plunged into the tasks of moving forward the housing and other projects; but from his first day on the job, he made it clear that he had no higher priority than the educational advancement of the tribe. It was not that he believed education was a cure-all for every Tigua problem. He had been through the system from first grade to graduate school, and he knew better than that. He knew, in fact, that the educational system could be a part of the Indian's problem.

Ray Apodaca is an articulate and plainspoken man when it comes to talking about Indians in America. "To most Americans, Indians are myths, legends, fairy tales," he says. "They see Indians in television movies or read a novel about them, and then put them back in the toy box and forget them. The overwhelming majority of Americans couldn't tell you anything about modern Indians and certainly nothing about their problems.

"And that includes most school administrators and teachers. You can't have an educational system that responds to Indian needs if the people who run the system don't understand Indians. Up to now what education has done or tried to do is separate the Indian from his culture, destroy his original self, his Indian self, and create a new person.

"The educational system chops off the Indian's roots, but he needs those roots, just as much as a tree needs them to stay alive. For the Indian the worst thing that can happen is to be isolated from his tribe. In the old days Indians punished the most serious crimes by exile. That was the most terrible sentence for an Indian: to be sent out into the world to wander by himself, to never be able to come back to his tribe.

"Yet for a hundred years education has tried to cut Indians off from their tribe, and that is probably the main reason Indians have always had the highest school dropout rates in the country.

"The Indian who does stay in the system and gets an education ends up belonging nowhere. To the outside world the educated Indian is an oddity. To the inside world—his own tribe—he is not an Indian any more."

Ray Apodaca smiles at those words. "I'm talking about myself, of course," he says.

But Ray knew the system and he knew his own people. He was sure that there was much that could be done and must be done. One of the first actions was to get funds from the Office of Indian Education in Washington to start an early childhood development center in the new community building on the Tigua Reservation. Children between the ages of two and five were eligible to attend, and the program was one that would give them a start in the social and learning skills that they would need in public school. They were also taught some history of the Tigua tribe and learned the ceremonial dances. The Cacique himself, the traditional tribal leader, came to the Center regularly to help teach the children Tigua songs and to tell stories of the Tigua past.

Tigua parents at first hesitated to bring their children to the Early Childhood Learning Center. It was a new thing and they were not sure about it, but the mothers came and watched, and slowly they brought their children. They saw that of the eight teachers in the Center six were young Tigua women, and the

Tigua youngsters get their first taste of learning in a reservation classroom in El Paso.

mothers learned that these Tigua teachers were all taking night courses in college to become better at their work.

Another kind of schooling was taking place on the Tigua Reservation. Again using Office of Indian Education funds, the tribe set up an adult education program in which faculty members from El Paso Community College came to the reservation to tutor Tiguas who had dropped out of school but who wanted to earn a high school diploma. After a slow start, a large number of Tiguas enrolled in this program and stayed in it, gaining confidence from the friendly, sympathetic environment. Some

of them, even while still in the high school completion program, entered CETA and other job-training programs in the El
Paso area.

But the big turnaround in education came when, in Ray
Apodaca's words, the Tiguas confronted the school system.
"The Early Childhood Education and the adult education programs were splendid," Ray says, "but the answer for the future
had to lie in the public school system. That's where our children had to go when they finished the program here on the
reservation. That's where our junior high and high school boys
and girls had to go.

"We went to the schools that Tigua students attend. We
talked to superintendents, principals, and teachers about the
school dropout problems as we saw them, the problems we
thought the schools could do something about. We wanted a
special counseling system, one that would involve outreach
counselors from the Tigua tribe. We wanted a program that
would build some understanding on the part of the schools'
staffs about Tiguas and why they want to stay Tiguas. We
wanted to do a little educating of our own. We asked them to
come to our pueblo and get to know us better.

"We haven't worked any miracles, but things got better
and they're still getting better. The dropout rate is down and
performance is up. We're on the way, I think."

TODAY the Tigua tribe of El Paso is very much alive. Their
housing complex has well over one hundred attractive adobe
units. Besides the community center, they have an old pueblo
museum, a health clinic, and other public buildings. There is a
large arts and crafts center featuring Tigua beadwork, weaving,
jewelry, and pottery. Their pottery is in the ancient pueblo
tradition, and older women potters of the tribe teach their skills

to the younger women. The center has a restaurant featuring spicy and pungent Tigua foods and fresh bread from adobe ovens. Because they are an urban tribe, they have a steady flow of visitors and tourists, which they encourage; but they do not let these commercial activities overwhelm their private lives and traditions as a pueblo tribe.

Ray Apodaca has recently been promoted to the position of Executive Director of the Texas Indian Commission, but he is still very much concerned with the Tigua tribe. "The tribe has a long way to go," he says, "but we're on the right road, and our educational program is going to keep us on that road right into the next century."

▲▲▲▲▲▲▲▲▲▲▲▲▲▲▲▲▲▲▲

9

The Unconquered

THROUGHOUT much of their history American Indians had no access to law courts or to the federal Congress and state legislatures which often made laws that took away Indian lands and freedom. Today the situation is different. Indians have won full access to the courts, and there is hardly a tribe that does not have some legal case in progress or in preparatory stages, cases involving land claims or compensation for lost land, protection of water rights, and the establishing of hunting and fishing rights.

The petitioning of Congress and state legislatures for new laws or changes in old ones affecting Indians takes place often. Federal and state regulations pertaining to Indians are under constant review. The *Handbook of Federal Indian Law* is over eight hundred pages.

Well-trained lawyers with Indian interests at heart have become essential to modern tribes, and tribal leaders are encouraging young Indians to enter the legal profession. In 1970 there were only about twenty Indian lawyers. Today there are more than two hundred. That number is still very small, but programs such as the American Indian Law Center at the University of New Mexico will bring about a more rapid increase.

Jim Shore of the Florida Seminoles is one of the growing number of young Indian lawyers. He is, in fact, the first member of his tribe to become a lawyer, but his story is much more than that of earning a law degree. It is a story that symbolizes the deep-rooted Indian determination to survive.

IN THE LONG and bitter annals of Indian wars, none was as costly to the United States in lives and money as the war against the Seminoles in Florida. Between 1835 and 1842, 1,500 federal and state troops were killed and over $20 million was spent in the government's trying to force the Seminoles to move west to what is now Oklahoma so that settlers could have the Indians' good Florida farmland. In the end the might of U.S. forces prevailed but not until the great Seminole leader Osceola was captured under a flag of truce and put into prison.

Even then the U.S. victory was not complete. A few hundred Seminoles refused to go West with the main body of the tribe and fled into the wilderness of the Everglades. In those swamps and marshes, the Seminoles lived in small groups, constantly on the move, subsisting on fish, game, and other foods that grew naturally. They were hunted like animals, and a bounty was paid for every Seminole killed or captured; still, they survived in their watery hiding place.

In 1842 the United States declared the war against the Seminoles over. It was simply too costly and too hard to try to kill or capture the small number that had sought refuge in the Everglades, and the government decided to let them remain as long as they were peaceful. There was a final period of fighting between 1855 and 1857, which ended when a brave chief named Billy Bowlegs agreed to go West with his family and 139 followers.

Generational change among the Seminoles. Here is a teenager and her grand-mother.

Still, a few Seminoles—perhaps no more than 150 men, women and children—refused to leave their Everglades sanctuary. They stayed on, a people apart, living their solitary lives, keeping their ancient customs. They asked help of no one and received none. They grew corn, pumpkins, and squash on tiny patches of land, and the wilderness provided the rest. They were healthy, even in the mosquito-infested swamps, and their numbers slowly increased.

The present-day Seminole Indians of Florida are descendants of those brave and hardy people. Well into the twentieth century the Seminoles continued to lead lives that were very isolated from the rest of Florida society. Seminole chiefs were so afraid of having tribal customs and culture weakened that, until the 1930s, they forbade Seminole children to attend any kind of formal schools. A truce between the United States government and the Seminoles was not signed until 1934.

But as this century has progressed, major changes have taken place. The Seminoles now have their own federal trust reservation totaling 79,000 acres. A large part of the reservation, Big Cypress, is in the heart of the Everglades. Another large part, called Brighton, is near Lake Okeechobee, and a tiny third portion, the 480-acre tribal headquarters, is contained inside the city limits of Hollywood near Miami Beach. Seminole children now attend Florida public schools. The differences between the isolated parts of the reservation at Big Cypress and Brighton and the city headquarters are like the differences between day and night, but the Seminoles remain a strong and united tribe.

JIM SHORE was born and raised on the reservation at Brighton. The Brighton Reservation's thirty-six-thousand acres are a mixture of sandy pastureland and swamps with cypress-forested hillocks. The people who live there do some vegetable

A Seminole teenager

farming, but the main activity is raising cattle and hogs. Jim's father, Frank Shore, was a cattle raiser and also one of the Seminole tribe's medicine men.

Jim grew up as a rather typical reservation boy. During his boyhood years his family, which included four sisters and two brothers, lived in chickees. The chickee, traditional dwelling place of the Seminoles, is a simple open-sided structure of cypress poles which support a roof made of palmetto palm fronds. Later the family moved into a modern, low-cost house, but that was after Jim was grown.

Jim fished and hunted in the swamps and forested hill-ocks, helped his father with the cattle, and went to high school in Okeechobee, the nearest large town to Brighton Reservation. He was a reasonably good student, played some football, and breathed a sigh of relief when he graduated. The idea of going to college never seriously entered his mind. As he saw his life after high school, he would stay on the reservation and become a cattle raiser like his father.

And then one evening, in the murky light of sundown, Jim Shore's life was changed forever in the shattering moment of a car wreck. Afterward Jim could never remember exactly what happened. He was driving; he did remember that. Suddenly another car was in front of him, and they were meeting head-on. Jim swerved, heard the crunch of fenders, felt his car hur-tling into the canal that ran beside the road. He slammed into the windshield.

When Jim regained consciousness, he was in a hospital, and the world was dark. He could not see.

From the hospital in the little town of Clewiston, where he was first taken, Jim was transferred that same night to a hospi-tal in West Palm Beach, and he was there for three weeks. There were no broken bones or internal injuries, but the force of impact and the windshield glass had done their cruel work on his eyes. The doctors spoke in terms of optic nerve and other damage that Jim could not understand, but no one would say when or if he would see again.

After his release from the hospital, Jim returned to the reservation, and what had been a good and comfortable world was now a place of darkness. For a young man who had spent a part of almost every day on horseback tending cattle, who had fished and prowled the wooded hillocks, sitting idly week after week, month after month was sheer physical pain. His family and friends were kind to him, but kindness could not fill

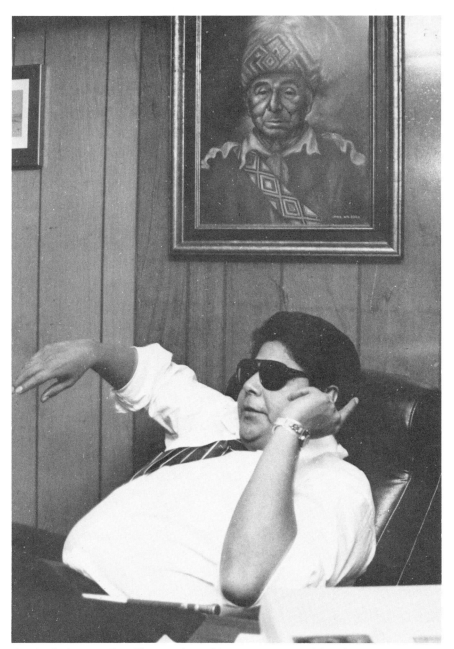

Seminole lawyer Jim Shore. Above him is a picture of his father wearing the traditional clothing of a medicine man.

the great black void of useless days, each one that seemed without end.

Three times between 1970 and 1973 Jim had eye operations. Each time he went into the hospital he told himself not to get his hopes too high, but after each failure the disappointment was there, hurting like a raw wound. After the third operation failed, the doctors knew and Jim knew that he would be blind for the rest of his life.

Jim cannot recall when, during those dark years, the idea of going to college first came into his head. "But it was my idea," Jim says. "Nobody suggested it to me. Except for my eyes, I was perfectly healthy, and the chances were that I would be around for a long time. I just couldn't handle the thought of sitting there on the reservation for forty or fifty years, not doing anything except being a burden to my family and my tribe."

In the fall of 1973, with financial support from the Florida Division of Blind Services, Jim enrolled in the North Florida Junior College in the town of Madison. He had learned braille, but his study, assignments, and tests were done almost entirely with cassettes. Study material and test questions would be put onto cassettes for him by readers, and he would do assignments and take tests in the same way.

"That extra help cost money," Jim says, "and I've always been grateful to the state."

After two years at the junior college, Jim decided that he had mastered the cassette method of study well enough to transfer to Stetson University in DeLand. Stetson is an old Florida school that Jim had heard good things about, and it was not a huge place like the University of Florida and Florida State. That was important to Jim. Stetson seemed a long way from Brighton Reservation, but he knew he had to make the break.

At Stetson Jim majored in American history, putting as

much emphasis as he could on Indians in the country's history. He lived alone in a dormitory; to the best of his knowledge, no other Indians were enrolled at the university while he was there. His life was totally focused on being a good student, and if he felt loneliness, homesickness, and self-doubts, he does not talk about that now.

"I was busy," he says. Was the intensity of his study in part a reaction to the years of enforced idleness on the reservation? It seems likely.

Although the study of history is a standard pre-law program, Jim insists that he had no long-range plan to become a lawyer. "I just couldn't figure out how a B.A. in history could help me or anyone else very much," he says, "so I decided to go to law school."

In 1977 Jim was admitted to the Stetson College of Law in St. Petersburg, Florida. Now his financial help from the state was supplemented by funds from the Seminole tribe. Jim embarked on a year-round study program, relying entirely on cassettes, and in 1980 he graduated, the first member of his tribe to hold a law degree.

Today Jim works at the Seminole tribal headquarters, using his knowledge of the law in the tribe's rapidly expanding legal concerns, which include land issues and several successful business ventures. The Seminoles also have their own police force, and Jim has helped it organize and define its role on the reservation.

On the wall behind Jim Shore's desk is a picture of his father wearing the traditional clothing of a Seminole medicine man. A visitor to Jim's office seeing that picture, seeing Jim sitting there, a practicing lawyer against all odds, cannot help seeing something else. He sees in this father and son the long history of the Seminoles, a people who were and still are determined not to give up, not to be conquered.

10

Tiger, Tiger

T H E Miccosukee Indians of Florida are closely related to
the Seminoles. They speak the same language, called
Mikasuki, and share most of the same customs and beliefs. Like the Seminoles, many of the Miccosukees refused to
be removed to Oklahoma during the early nineteenth century
and withstood the same terrible hardships of living like hunted
animals in the Everglades. But the Miccosukees have always
had their own leaders and blood relationships and think of
themselves as a tribe separate from the Seminoles.

If possible, the Miccosukees—who number only about five
hundred men, women, and children—have guarded their freedom even more fiercely than the Seminoles. When the Seminole tribe signed a truce with the United States in 1934, the
Miccosukees refused to join in the signing, and they have
never to this day concluded a treaty with the government.

In 1961 the Miccosukees adopted a constitution and by-
laws in order to meet a legal requirement for recognition as a
tribe by the federal government. Even then a number of indi-

vidual Miccosukees refused to sign the tribal role because they did not want to be part of an official organization. Legally, therefore, they are not members of the tribe although they are certainly Miccosukees.

Today, through a special government permit, the Miccosukees live just inside Everglades National Park on a strip of land five hundred feet wide and five-and-a-half miles long. Along this narrow ribbon of firm earth, through the Everglade swamps that have been called some of the wildest in America, runs Highway 41 which connects Miami in the east with Naples, Florida, in the west. The highway is known as the Tamiami Trail, and the Miccosukees are sometimes called Trail Indians.

From this tiny land base, only thirty-seven miles from Miami, the Miccosukees fish and hunt the seemingly endless acres of watery saw grass and wooded cypress knolls that surround them, much as their ancestors did. Yet these same people have entered into the life of the late twentieth century in the most astonishing way. Nearly all of them now live in small modern houses instead of chickees, a traditional open-sided shelter. Their children go to a good school run by the tribe, although only twenty-five years ago few Miccosukees received any formal education.

Avoiding contact with whites had been a Miccosukee way of life since the early nineteenth century, but today all outsiders are welcome regardless of skin color. The tribe runs a restaurant where visitors and travelers along the Tamiami Trail can find good food, including Indian dishes. There is a service station and a shop stocked with the traditional arts and crafts of the Miccosukees and other Indian tribes. There is an Indian village with a cooking chickee, sleeping chickees, and working chickees, typical of a family camp of earlier days. Miccosukee guides are available to take adventurous visitors deep into the Everglades by boat.

The outside world can now share some elements of Miccosukee life, just as most Miccosukees are sharing the life beyond their Everglades home by living in modern houses, going to school, paying income taxes, obtaining drivers' licenses, and shopping in Miami supermarkets.

LEE AND STEPHEN TIGER cannot be called typical young Miccosukees, but they have shared the experience of their tribe in adjusting to a lifeway that includes both the white and Indian worlds. In their case, however, their Indian and tribal identity developed most strongly later in their lives. First they lived very much in the white world.

Lee and Stephen are brothers, sons of Buffalo Tiger, who has been Chairman of the Miccosukee tribe since it was recognized by the government in 1962. More than any other person, Buffalo Tiger led the Miccosukees into the modern world, while at the same time helping them win a piece of land in the Everglades and come together there to protect their tribal traditions.

The Tiger family lived in Miami because that was where Buffalo Tiger could most effectively carry on the work of trying to get government recognition for the Miccosukee tribe. Lee and Stephen knew about their Indian background and about what their father was doing for the Miccosukee tribe's future, but all of that did not have a great importance to them as they were growing up. Sometimes they went with their father to visit Miccosukee groups in the Everglades, however, and they learned about their people in that way.

But for the most part they grew up like typical Miami suburban boys, little different from their white and Hispanic school companions. In high school they became absorbed in rock music, Lee learning to play the guitar, bass, and piano,

Lee Tiger

Stephen concentrating on the guitar. While still in high school they formed their own rock group with the name Tiger, Tiger.

After high school, music dominated their lives. Their rock group began to get engagements in local clubs and performed in Miami rock concerts. Both Lee and Stephen were featured singers for the group. Stephen wrote the words and music for many of the group's songs, and Lee did the arranging. Tiger, Tiger was not exactly a household name, but in Miami they were becoming known.

And then Lee Tiger, with his singing and his unusual range of musical instruments, was invited to join a New York rock group. It would be a step up and widen Lee's experience

Miccosukee artist, Stephen Tiger

in the music business. Even though it meant breaking up Tiger, Tiger, Stephen told his brother that he should not pass up the chance. Lee did join the group and spent a year performing in New York and other eastern cities. It was fun, and he learned new things about the artistic and business sides of rock music, just as he and Stephen hoped he would.

In the meantime, Stephen was exercising another talent he had discovered early in life but that had taken second place to his interest in music. He began painting seriously. A self-taught artist, Stephen studied the work of other painters, sketched, experimented in various media: oils, watercolors, tempera. He even turned to sculpture as a means of increasing his sense of form. Like Lee in New York, Stephen was having a year of learning in Miami.

Then the New York rock group decided to break up. Lee thought about returning to Miami, but the final decision was quite different. The two brothers decided that Stephen would come to New York and that they would reform Tiger, Tiger there. For Stephen it would mean not only returning to music but also having the opportunity to see and study the richness of the New York art world.

They recruited two other musicians, and Tiger, Tiger was alive again, over a thousand miles from its Miami birthplace. The rock music business is tough and competitive, but the group managed enough bookings to keep themselves together, and it was in New York that Lee and Stephen cut their first long-play album. The disc was recorded for and released by ESP Records, and, as Lee recalls, "It was great to have all that big-time back-up."

The name of the album was *Eye of the Tiger* and, it should be noted, was made years before a Chicago rock group The Survivors recorded a song with that same title, which became famous as the theme of the movie *Rocky III*. The Survivors later released an album entitled *Eye of the Tiger*. Except for having the same title, The Survivors' album and song have nothing to do with Lee and Stephen's earlier album.

When a West Coast promoter offered to arrange a series of bookings for them, the Tiger, Tiger group moved to Los Angeles. They played West Coast cities for a year, and then Lee and Stephen decided that it was time to return to Miami. They had enjoyed New York and California, and for young men still in their early twenties, they had learned a great deal about both the artistic and business sides of being professional musicians.

They were still interested in making music a major part of their lives, but other things were stirring in them. Stephen wanted more time for his painting, and they had had a request from their father that was very much on their minds. Buffalo Tiger had freely let his sons pursue their careers, but now he asked them to step back to take a look at themselves as Miccosukees and to take a look at what was happening to their tribe.

Good things were happening. Most Miccosukees had now come from Miami or scattered places in the Everglades to live on their small reservation. Although some people still lived in chickees, more and more modern low-cost houses were being built. The restaurant, service station, and grocery store that had been built before Lee and Stephen left were making money and providing jobs for Miccosukees. An elementary school and a health clinic had been started on the reservation, as had a Head Start program for young children and an adult education program featuring reading, writing, and arithmetic.

Buffalo Tiger showed his sons these things and asked them to consider entering into the life of the Miccosukees. Without any idea of how long they would keep at it, Lee and Stephen decided to turn at least part of their attention toward their tribe. But what could they do? Considering their backgrounds as rock musicians and, in Stephen's case, artist, how could they fill some need of the tribe? The answers proved to be in those very backgrounds.

The Miccosukees needed to increase the volume of tourism to their reservation attractions. Lee's experience in publicizing Tiger, Tiger, in obtaining bookings, in dealing with newspapers, television, and radio proved to be very transferable to dealing with the publicity needs of the tribe. Quickly Lee found himself giving full time to public relations and promotional programs for the tribe.

Stephen also gave some time to public relations, but not on a regular basis. He soon discovered, however, that his ability as an artist could be used by the tribe in a number of ways: preparing publicity materials, doing drawings picturing the Miccosukee tribe in history for the tribal museum, doing paintings to be used for special occasions, even for the tribal Christmas card. While continuing to paint and sell on his own, Stephen became the unofficial artist for the Miccosukee tribe.

There was no Tiger, Tiger rock group now, but music was never far from either Lee's or Stephen's minds. As the months passed, Stephen began to write songs again, but the songs were markedly different from those he had written in the past. Their work with the tribe had brought Lee and Stephen close to their Miccosukee heritage for the first time. They were getting to know the people, becoming familiar with their thoughts, hopes, and ambitions, getting to see and feel the Miccosukee way of life.

Many of the songs that Stephen wrote during this period were a reflection of what he and Lee were learning about their people and about themselves as Indians, as Miccosukees. The music was still rock, but the themes of the songs were about the Indians of the Everglades, both today and in the past: songs with such titles as "This Is My Country" and "Not the Last Red

Man." "We Won't Be Leaving" is a celebration of the great Seminole leader Osceola and the resistance of the Florida Indians to removal to Oklahoma.

One of the songs, "River of Grass," combines a powerful ecological statement with some beautiful word images. It tells of a young Everglades Indian many years ago:

> *Pushed my canoe down into the river of grass,*
> *Made my home on an island in the river of grass . . .*
> *Grew some food, hunted for the meat that I ate,*
> *Fished in the river, the crystal clear river,*
> *Swam in the sun upon the lake . . .*

The song then moves to the present or perhaps the future, and the man, no longer young, looks for an egret in the sky, but the spirits of the vanished Everglades creatures cry out to him,

> *You can find us on a postcard,*
> *Taken maybe forty-five years ago.*

For two years Lee and Stephen made time in busy schedules for their music, worked on it, thought about it, talked about it. And then they agreed that it was time to bring Tiger, Tiger back to life for the third time. They recruited two additional musicians, a lead guitarist and a drummer, and began to take engagements in the Miami area.

The guitarist and the drummer are not Indians. "We never have tried to make Tiger, Tiger an all-Indian group," Lee says. "That isn't the idea at all. We just want to make the best music we can with the best talent available. If that happened to be Indian talent, that's what we'd have playing with us."

Today Lee and Stephen Tiger are very busy young men. Lee is the full-time Public Information and Marketing Manager for the Miccosukee tribe. Stephen is increasingly successful with his painting, receiving commissions and having exhibitions. He continues to be the tribe's artist, and he has received a grant from the state to further his work.

Sometimes Lee and Stephen both undertake public relations work. In 1982 they went to Spain with a group promoting tourism in Florida. Lee and Stephen took along an alligator to symbolize the wildlife of the Everglades. The creature made a big hit, and when they donated it to a zoo, the King and Queen came to see it.

The Tiger brothers found that they were also the focus of considerable attention. "Europeans are interested in American Indians," Lee says. "We tried to tell them about our very special Miccosukee tribe that lives in the Everglades, but I don't know how successful we were. To them, Indians are Indians. But maybe we started to change that notion, especially when we played some rock music."

Lee and Stephen are still playing rock, scheduling Tiger, Tiger into night clubs not only in Miami but other southern cities as well. Sometimes they play for Indian fairs or festivals, and then their music has a special meaning. Doing their regular work by day and their rock performances several times a month at night is a demanding routine that leaves almost no time for leisure. But they are doing things they love to do and living their lives fully.

In January, 1983, the Miccosukees' long fight for some measure of justice came to an end when Congress settled their land claim by giving them 190,000 acres of Everglade land. Congress also awarded the tribe almost one million dollars as a part of the settlement. The Miccosukees have long-range plans to use their new land for aquaculture, agricultural development in certain areas, and additional tourism projects. A statement by the tribe about their land clearly underscores one of their major goals: "The Miccosukees hope to demonstrate to non-Indians how man can remain in touch with nature and still humanize his environment."

Lee and Stephen Tiger expect to be a part of the tribe's future development work. They know now that they are very much a part of the tribe. On one weekend they can go deep into an isolated spot in the Everglades to take part in the Green Corn Dance, an ancient ceremony by which Miccosukees renew themselves as Indians in communion with nature. The next weekend Lee and Stephen may be playing rock music in Miami or Atlanta. But wherever they are, they know who they are and where they belong. They know they are Miccosukees.

11

The City Dwellers

ONLY 50 percent of all American Indians live on reservations. Of the other half, the majority make their homes in large cities, either temporarily or permanently. Some cities have Indian populations larger than those of most reservations. Almost fifty thousand Indians from over seventy different tribes live in Los Angeles, for example. Oklahoma City's Indian residents number over twenty-five thousand. Large numbers of Indians live in such cities as Chicago, Detroit, Phoenix, Albuquerque, Seattle, and Denver, to name but a few. It is probable that every American city has some Indian residents.

Many Indian families have lived in cities for generations, but the great influx from the reservations to urban areas is relatively recent. During the Eisenhower administration, government policy was to try to end the federal trust relationship with Indian tribes and "assimilate" Indians into the white culture. Government obligations to over one hundred Indian tribes were terminated from 1954 to 1962; thousands of Indians were encouraged to leave their tribal lands and go to live in cities.

Ted Risingsun was living on the Northern Cheyenne Reservation in Montana at that time, and he remembers well the efforts of the Bureau of Indian Affairs to break up tribal life. "People from the BIA talked to us, mostly the younger ones like me, about leaving the reservation and going out where the jobs were," he recalls. "They said Indians ought to get into what they called the mainstream of American life and not hide away by themselves on a reservation.

"The BIA made it real easy for an Indian to leave the reservation. The government had what they called relocation centers in some of the big cities. When we had picked a place we wanted to go, the BIA gave us travel expenses and money to live on for the first month while we looked for a job. The relocation center was supposed to help us get settled and find work."

Ted Risingsun went to St. Louis, did not get the promised help from the relocation center, but found a job on his own. He lived in St. Louis for several years, and then, like many others who try the urban experience, returned to make his life on the reservation.

But thousands stayed in the cities; and although the government has again changed its policy and no longer encourages Indians to leave their reservations, thousands still do make the move to cities every year. Most of them are young because the main reasons Indians come to urban areas are to continue their education and to look for jobs. How can young Indians, whose cultural roots may not yet be deeply set, retain their tribal identity in the city? How can those who were born in the city be Indians in anything but name?

"Some stop being Indians or never are Indians in anything

but name," says a young Kiowa man who works for an oil well equipment company in Oklahoma City. "Of course, that's true. But you can be an Indian in the city if you want to be, and I think most do want to be. We have a history and a culture that is ours, just ours, whether we are Kiowas, Comanches, Chickasaws, or whatever. We don't want to lose that. We don't want to be dark-skinned white people."

"But it is wrong to think we spend all our time sitting around thinking about being Indians," adds a Pawnee member of an Oklahoma City accounting firm, whose wife is also Pawnee. "We don't. There is too much else to do. My wife and I both work; she sells real estate. We're buying our first house and making payments on furniture and a car. We're busy with the everyday things of life, just like everyone else. But we take part in Pawnee and other Indian activities in Oklahoma City and other places—powwows, festivals, things like that. We know the history of our tribe. We have lots of Pawnee friends. We're Pawnees but we do non-Indian things every day, and we don't get confused."

At least forty-three cities in the United States have Indian centers which have been started and developed by the Indian residents of those cities. The primary purpose of most of the centers is to help newly arrived Indians, usually from reservations or small rural communities, in their adjustment to city life. They help newcomers find housing and they have lists of possible employers. They explain the city transportation systems and sometimes help with legal problems which come up too often for persons unacquainted with city laws and regulations.

The centers usually also have social programs in which Indians of all tribes take part: dances, songfests, dinners featuring Indian foods. These centers provide not only important settling-in services but also a valuable ongoing means by which

Balerma Burgess, Comanche

Indian city dwellers from different tribes can get to know more about each other.

Balerma Burgess is a Comanche Indian who was born in a small Oklahoma town. Her father was a construction worker, and early in her life her family moved to Denver and then to Dallas. There were very few Indians in the schools that she went to, and Balerma remembers feeling out of place and inadequate.

The organization of an Indian center in Dallas, in which

her mother was very active, made a big difference for Balerma. She met and shared experiences with Indian teenagers of many tribes. From the center's activities she learned more about herself as an Indian and gained a measure of self-confidence that she previously had not had. She became one of the youth leaders of the center, and after graduation from high school returned to her native state to take a degree from Oklahoma State University.

Today Balerma lives in the small city of Norman, where the University of Oklahoma is located. She works in the education division of Oklahomans for Indian Opportunity. "I do talent search," she says, "looking for Indian high school students who are good prospects for college, motivating them, helping to get them ready when necessary."

She credits her mother's strength and the Indian center in Dallas with giving her the help she needed at a critical time in her life. "I still have pangs of being inadequate," she says with a smile, "but they aren't strong enough to keep me from going to a good graduate school for a master's in management. That's my next goal."

Indians in some cities come together in groups primarily for companionship, for the chance to express themselves as Indians, and for the opportunity for their children to be in an Indian atmosphere. The American Indian Society of Washington, D.C., is an excellent example of such an organization. Mitchell Bush, an Onondaga Indian from New York and an employee of the Bureau of Indian Affairs, is current president of the Society. He says about it:

"Indians have been working in Washington since the forties, but more of us started arriving here in the sixties because the BIA began a real effort to recruit Indians for jobs. Washington was a big and strange city to us. We wanted an Indian fellowship, and we wanted a way to keep our tribal traditions

A group of urban Indians that meets regularly in suburban Washington, D.C.

An urban Indian plays his drum for the group to practice Indian dances.

alive. So we started the American Indian Society. That was in 1966, and there were maybe twenty or thirty of us in the founding group. Most of us were young.

"Today the Society has over three hundred members belonging to sixty-five different tribes. Over the past seventeen years it really has become a family organization. Parents and children and even grandparents take part. It still provides the Indian fellowship we were looking for, and it gives our children a chance to see themselves as Indians and do Indian things."

The American Indian Society of Washington has a lively program. It sponsors powwows in Washington to which Indians come from all over the country. It sends dance troupes of its own members to take part in powwows in other cities. A favorite event is the annual Thanksgiving Day dinner where all Indian foods are served.

"Of course, we have turkey," says one member. "Turkey was an Indian food before white people ever heard of it."

A major accomplishment of the Society was the purchase of forty-six acres of unimproved timberland in Virginia, less than two hours' drive from Washington. The land has been named Indian Pines, and it is a wonderful refuge where Society members can go to camp for a weekend or a long vacation. The campers can harvest berries, sassafras roots, nuts, persimmons, and holly, and the children get some sense of the lives that many of their parents and grandparents lived on reservations.

"We make our own money for everything we do," explains Mitchell Bush. "We don't get a cent from the govenment or any other organization. We put out and sell a beautiful Indian calendar and an Indian cookbook with recipes contributed by Society members. We have a food booth at most of the local fairs and festivals put on by other ethnic groups, like the His-

Audrey Black Bull Wolff, a Sioux, having a reflective moment at the University of Arizona where she is studying accounting.

panics. We sell Indian foods, and things like fry bread, Indian tacos, and Iroquois corn soup are always big hits. We make money, and it is fun to introduce people to Indian food."

Indian dances are practiced at regular monthly meetings in members' homes. Children learn to dance, and adult members learn the dances of tribes other than their own. Indian arts and crafts nights are held regularly, too, where both children and adults can learn beadwork, leathercraft, and jewelry making.

"An Indian in the city doesn't have to forget who he is," says one member of the Society, "unless he wants to."

Many Indians who live in cities keep a link to their tribal heritage for themselves and their children by making regular visits back to their reservation. Such a person is Audrey Black Bull Wolff, a Sioux Indian who grew up on the Crow Creek Reservation in South Dakota. She now lives in Tucson where both she and her husband are students at the University of Arizona. "I always want to live near Indians so that I can participate in Indian life," she says. "I try to go home every summer for two months, and I take my son. He thinks of himself as a Sioux. I never feel as though I'm leaving the reservation for good. I'm just away for a while. Crow Creek is my home."

Being an Indian in a city clearly means different things to different people, depending on their individual circumstances. But a high school senior, a Choctaw who was born and raised in Memphis, Tennessee, seemed to sum up what most urban Indians probably feel when he said, "Being an Indian is just one part of my life, but it is a part that is important to me."

▲▲▲▲▲▲▲▲▲▲▲▲▲▲▲▲▲▲

12

Washington, D.C., Native Americans' Capital

INDIANS have been coming to Washington, D.C., almost from the time the city became the capital of the country in 1791. For many decades they came for one reason: to plead with Congress, with the Commissioner of Indian Affairs, with the Great Father himself, as some called the president, for justice for their tribes. The promises of fair treatment given in Washington were many, the broken promises almost as many.

The names of Indian leaders of the nineteenth century who made the usually disappointing journey to Washington read like an honor roll of Indian history: Joseph, brilliant Nez Perce war chief whose greatest desire was for peace; Red Cloud, a great Sioux leader who also strove for peace but who fought so well when he was forced to that the U.S. Army named a whole campaign for him. They called it the Red Cloud War. Little Robe and War Bonnet of the Cheyennes, Spotted Wolf and Neva of the Arapahoes, White Bull of the Kiowas, Ten Bears of the Comanches: The list of chiefs who went to the nation's capital for talks could go on and on.

One of the most eloquent speeches in American history was delivered by Chief Joseph in Washington in 1879 when he spoke to a large group of government officials to explain the needs of his people and to ask for justice. His closing words were these:

> Whenever the white man treats an Indian as they treat each other, then we will have no more wars. We shall all be alike— brothers of one father and one mother, with one sky above us and one country around us, and one government for all. Then the Great Spirit Chief who rules above will smile upon this land, and send rain to wash out the bloody spots made by brothers' hands from the face of the earth. For this time the Indian race are waiting and praying. I hope that no more groans of wounded men and women will ever go to the ear of the Great Spirit Chief above, and that all people may be one people.

Today Indian leaders are still coming to Washington to work for the welfare of their tribes. Now they arrive at National Airport with briefcases bulging and often accompanied by a tribal lawyer. As in the past, they see members of Congress, the Commissioner of Indian Affairs, and occasionally the president, who is no longer called the Great Father. But most of their time in Washington is spent with officials in the departments of Interior, Health and Human Services, Labor, and Justice. They are still seeking justice, but now their talks center on land claims, water rights, funds for education, and economic development programs for their reservations.

Most of these leaders now carry the title of tribal chairman, governor, or president instead of chief. Some have very Indian-sounding names like Buffalo Tiger, Chairman of the Miccosukees, and Delbert Horsechief, President of the Pawnees. Others have names like Allen Rowland, Chairman of the Northern Cheyenne, and Phillip Martin, head of the Mississippi Band of Choctaws, who still carries the traditional title of chief. But whatever their names, all are Indians.

The number of Indians living in Washington, D.C., cannot compare with the large Indian populations of such cities as Los Angeles, Minneapolis, and Oklahoma City. The 1980 census shows just over one thousand Indians living in Washington; if the Maryland and Virginia suburbs are included, that number probably would go well beyond two thousand. But in this city numbers do not tell the story.

What happens in Washington is crucial to almost all Indians in America. During every term of Congress from fifty to one hundred bills having to do with all Indians or with individual tribes will be acted on. Headquarters for the Bureau of Indian Affairs is in Washington. Also located here are the Office of Indian Education and the Administration for Native Americans, both important government organizations. The Department of Labor has a Division of Indian and Native American Programs based in Washington.

The large majority of Indians who live and work in Washington, for either long periods or short, are concerned with Indian matters. Over two hundred of the Bureau of Indian Affairs' 350 Washington employees are Indians, a great change from earlier times when hardly any Indians worked there. Since 1966 every Commissioner of Indian Affairs has been an Indian. Before 1966 only one Indian, Ely Samuel Parker, a member of the Seneca tribe of New York, had been Commissioner. That was in 1869.

A number of nongovernment Indian organizations are located in Washington. Their activities differ, but in general they are all focused on the same thing: an improved way of life for America's Indians. The National Congress of American Indians, for example, monitors all new developments in legislation and government policy affecting Indians and keeps the tribes informed. It also takes recommendations from the tribes and sees that they are presented effectively to government officials and members of Congress. Over 150 tribes belong to the NCAI. The Indian Law Resource Center has a small group of lawyers that helps tribes in the courts with their land claims. The Council of Energy Resource Tribes gives Washington representation and many other services to over twenty western tribes that have coal, oil, natural gas, uranium, or oil shale resources on their reservation lands.

With organizations like these and with the Bureau of Indian Affairs headquarters, Washington is a magnet that draws young Indians to it. Some come as interns to work in summer jobs, sometimes as a part of their college programs. One of the main purposes of such programs is to give the intern knowledge about what is going on in Washington to advance Indian welfare and development. It is not unusual for an intern to return to Washington to work after he or she has completed college.

The Indian organizations in Washington are always on the lookout for young Indian men and women whose educational backgrounds and experience equip them for work in this very special city. Such a person is Elizabeth Lohah, a young Osage Indian who is Deputy Director of the Washington-based Americans for Indian Opportunity.

The Osage, southern cousins of the Sioux, once ranged over a vast part of middle America and claimed all of what is now Arkansas and much other land west of the Missouri River. Today the Osage live on about two hundred thousand acres of individually allotted land in northeastern Oklahoma, and it was there that Elizabeth grew up. She lived with her mother, father, and brothers on a farm near the little town of Hominy, where she went to school.

Her early years were rather typical ones for an Osage girl growing up in the sixties. She went to school in Hominy, riding the school bus with other Osage children who lived in the

Elizabeth Lohah

country. Most of the students in the school were white, but there was a large Indian minority. Elizabeth took part in school activities, belonged to the Girl Scouts, and was a member of the All-Indian Bowling League.

Very early she learned Osage dances and went with her family to Osage powwows and celebrations that were held in the Indian communities of the towns of Hominy, Gray Horse, and Pawhuska, where the Osage tribal headquarters is located. She went to festive dinners where good Osage food such as fry bread, grape dumplings, and beef steam-fry were served, and she took part in other solemn meals where neighbors and friends from all over brought food to share with Osage families who had had sons killed in Vietnam.

Elizabeth learned about her clan and received her clan name Heatome, which is pronounced He-ah-tow-may. Osage children are taught by their parents, relatives, and tribal elders to be proud of being an Osage, and Elizabeth received this instruction. She remembers being told stories of Osage courage and intelligence.

"We were told over and over that Osages are handsome and tall," she says. "Being part of a good family is very important and something to take great pride in." And she adds, "My great-grandfather was an Osage chief."

Although Elizabeth lived on a farm, her father was not a farmer but rather a lawyer, a graduate of the Tulsa University Law School, and also an elected judge. In 1972 he was asked to come to Washington to be part of a special presidential task force to study Indian policy for the Nixon administration. He took his family with him, so at the age of fourteen Elizabeth found herself uprooted from her pleasant, familiar rural, small town Oklahoma life and transported to the totally strange world of suburban Washington, D.C.

"The first shock was the noise," Elizabeth remembers. "The thousands of cars filling the streets day and night, the police sirens, the fire trucks. I was used to going to sleep on the farm hearing nothing but crickets and maybe an oil well pumping in the distance."

The real shock, however, was the huge suburban high school that Elizabeth went to. "Hominy High School was very conservative," she says. "I couldn't believe how these big city kids dressed and how long the boys wore their hair. In Hominy even the Indian boys cut their hair short, although, of course, the sixties soon changed that.

"The kids in the school teased me, not because I was an Indian but because of my Oklahoma accent. They would try to imitate the way I talked. They would say things like, 'She's from a ra-n-ch in Oklahoma,' making ranch come out in three syllables. That's the way I sounded to them, I guess.

"There was a big black girl who thought I was white and decided she didn't like me. I think it was because I was from Oklahoma. One day she pushed me into a corner and started screaming at me. She said she was going to beat me up. I was still new in school and afraid of just about everything, but having her yell at me that she was going to beat me up because I was white really made me mad. I started screaming at her that I was an Osage Indian, and I threatened her with my own brand of Indian mayhem. I'm sure she wasn't afraid, but she was so amazed that I was an Indian that she backed right off. In fact, she soon decided that she liked me and would be my protector."

But Elizabeth did not need protection. She did well in the Washington suburban school, and when she was sixteen, she went to the University of Colorado, even before high school graduation, through the university's early acceptance program.

The University of Colorado, like Arizona State University, the University of Oklahoma, and several others, has a very fine program to help Indian students adjust to university life. There is an Indian club, special Indian activities and courses, and individual and group counseling for Indian students.

"I think programs like that are great," says Elizabeth. "They are a big help for young Indians who are often out of their tribal environment for the first time. They are a useful substitute for the support system that a tribe provides its young people. I know that the program at Colorado helped me, even though I wasn't exactly fresh off the reservation."

Elizabeth graduated from the University of Colorado with a degree in political science. "There is hardly anything more important for American Indian tribes today than to understand how the political and legal processes of this country work," she says. "I learned that early from my father and from other Indian leaders and activists I met. I was active in campus politics. The Indians and Hispanics at the University teamed up to try to win student government offices. We weren't very successful, but I learned a lot."

After graduation Elizabeth went to work for the Osage Nation Federal Programs Office in Pawhuska. "It was really good to be back with Osage people and in Osage country again," she says. "I could see my relatives in Hominy on weekends and take part in the special feasts and dances. I love our Osage dances."

Elizabeth's first job in the tribal office was to counsel Osages who wanted to enter the CETA program, a federally funded program which provides job training and help in finding employment. Later she became a program analyst, making sure that the terms of government projects for the Osage tribe were complied with and doing program evaluation.

"I had been warned by lots of educated Indians not to expect to be welcomed back to the tribe as a fountain of knowledge just because I had gone away and got an education. I was told that there might be jealousies and misunderstandings, that acceptance might come slowly. But it wasn't that way. I was accepted, and I didn't feel all the hostility I was warned to expect. I really think that the tribes—the Osage tribe anyway—are not only getting more used to the idea of their people going away to college but truly want them to come home."

Elizabeth worked in the tribal headquarters at Pawhuska for a year, and then came an invitation she couldn't refuse. The Council of Energy Resource Tribes in Washington, D.C., wanted her to join their staff as a research associate in public policy as it related to Indian-owned oil, natural gas, coal, and other energy reserves.

"I didn't want to leave Pawhuska," Elizabeth says, "but I couldn't pass up the chance to do that kind of work in Washington. It was right in line with my college studies, and it was a chance to learn about other tribes and about Indian programs from the government side."

Sometimes opportunities come close together. Elizabeth had been working at the Council of Energy Resource Tribes for just over a year when LaDonna Harris, President of Americans for Indian Opportunity, moved her organization from Albuquerque to Washington. She knew Elizabeth and her work and offered her a job in the new Washington office.

LaDonna Harris, a Comanche, is a dynamic and nationally known political activist who has long been a forceful speaker for human rights in general and Indian rights in particular. She created Americans for Indian Opportunity in 1970 and has received strong public and private support for its information, training, and research programs focused on Indian economic and cultural advancement.

"I liked what I was doing for CERT," says Elizabeth, "but I couldn't pass up the opportunity of working with LaDonna. It was an easy decision."

Today Elizabeth is absorbed in the activities of Americans

Elizabeth Lohah, right, shares a light moment with LaDonna Harris in the Washington office of Americans for Indian Opportunity.

for Indian Opportunity, which are concentrated on the continued progress of Indian tribal governments toward self-government and self-sufficiency. A study of a number of tribes is being carried out under an interagency contract with the Bureau of Indian Affairs and the Administration for Native Americans. The contract calls for AIO to assess the impact of government self-determination policies of the last decade on tribal governments and to evaluate their progress toward self-government. Most important, AIO is looking for opportunities to speed and strengthen self-government and to help tribes learn from each other's successes and mistakes.

Elizabeth is happy with her work and life in Washington. She travels a good deal, visiting tribes that AIO is working with. She likes her apartment which is within walking distance of her office, and her life is not unlike that of thousands of other young career women. "Except," she says with a smile, "when I go out with friends in the evening it is more likely to be to Indian hangouts like Bronco Billy's or Gary's Restaurant."

Elizabeth is not entirely certain about the future. "I like what I'm doing and I think it is important," she says, "but I think about going to law school. And I think that someday I might like to go back and work with my tribe again. Right now I just don't know, but I still have plenty of time to decide."

One thing Elizabeth is very certain of. "I know I can always go back to my tribe if I want to or need to," she says. "There is a strong support structure in the Osage tribe and all other Indian tribes, I think. Everyone is related to almost everyone else in some sort of way. There is the immediate family, of course, but the much larger family of aunts, uncles, cousins, nephews, nieces, grandparents, and the clan family beyond that. They all feel responsibility for each other. The extended family is very much a reality.

"I know I have a base in Hominy. No matter what Thomas Wolfe said, you can go home again. At least you can if you are an Indian, or in my case an Osage. I can go home anytime I want to and know that there is a place for me. That means I can take bigger risks, job risks and other kinds, in the nontribal world, the outside world, because I always have my tribe to go back to. I can just get on a plane and go back. I have a built-in security."

Elizabeth sums up her thoughts in this way, "Indians do have to live in two worlds, but that can be a source of strength and the basis for a richer, more interesting life."

▲▲▲▲▲▲▲▲▲▲▲▲▲▲▲▲▲▲

13

"I Know Who I Am"

T HE CULTURAL SECURITY that Elizabeth Lohah found
in her Osage background is totally different from the
confusion and conflict that many Indians have experienced as they try to adjust to life in a dominant white culture.
Yet, like Elizabeth, more and more young Indians today are
developing confidence in their Indian heritage. They can be
found on reservations, in schools and universities, and in cities
throughout the country.

Better and more enlightened education for Indians doubt-
less has brought about important changes in their self-image.
More than anything, however, the ability to remain confidently
an Indian while surrounded by a non-Indian culture has to do
with individual pride, toughness of mind and spirit, and an
unwavering belief that the Indian way of life is a good way of
life.

René Cochise is one who has those qualities in generous
measure. She is a great-great-great-granddaughter of Cochise,

René Cochise, Mescalero Apache

the almost legendary Apache leader who, together with
Geronimo, fought both the Mexican and U.S. governments
fiercely for many years in Arizona and New Mexico during the
nineteenth century. René was born on the Mescalero Apache
Reservation in southern New Mexico and grew up there during
the sixties. Her first language was Apache, and she did not
learn English until she started to school.

Today René is an intern working with The Council on the
Aging in Washington, D.C. Her office in the Council's L'Enfant
Plaza headquarters is practically at the foot of Capitol Hill, and
the great government buildings, the monuments, the parks are
her everyday sights in this very special city. When René talked
recently about the road she has traveled from the reservation to
Washington and where the road may lead in the future, this is
what she said:

When I was small my life was totally an Indian life. Our family was large and very poor, so much of the time I stayed with my grandmother. She lived in a part of the reservation called White Tail, and she lived in a tent. The tribe had given her a tiny one-room house, but she refused to stay in it and had the tent pitched right beside it. She had always lived in a tent. She had been born in Oklahoma where the Apaches were being held as prisoners by the government. She was a small girl when the tribe finally was given a reservation and allowed to return to New Mexico.

I loved living in the tent with my grandmother. She cooked outdoors in an old wheelbarrow, and I can still remember the wonderful food—fry bread and cornmeal mush that she would put Indian spices and sometimes chopped dried meat in. She roasted what we called Indian banana—I think it was a long, yellow squash—and she made milk gravy to eat with everything.

Sometimes she cooked mescal. Mescal is the pulp of a great desert flower, and it used to be the staple food of our band of the Apache tribe. In fact, Mescalero means "mescal maker." Mescal is very hard to find now, and no one eats it except during the big feast in July.

The Mescalero Apache Reservation is the most beautiful place I have ever seen. It is in the Sacramento Mountains and has some of the highest peaks in the whole Southwest. My friends and I played in the pine forests and the cold streams, and sometimes we looked for berries and nuts on the mountain slopes.

I learned about the religion of my people, about the Mountain God Dancer, from my grandmother and from elders of the tribe who teach children about those things. The Mescalero Apaches are divided into three groups, the green dancers, the yellow dancers, and the black-and-white dancers. I belong to the black-and-white dancers. Four times a year we would go to the sacred place for my group near the base of Sierra Blanca for ceremonies. There would be prayers for the people and for the land and things in nature. Feasts and dances were a part of the ceremonies.

I guess I make life on the reservation sound like paradise, but, of course, it wasn't. So many people were poor then. When I was just a baby, my family moved to San Francisco. That was during the time that the government was trying to get Indians to leave their reservations and take jobs in cities. My father was given training to be a barber. I don't really remember anything about living in the city, but it didn't work out at all. After a year we moved back to the reservation.

Most of the time my father did not have a job, but sometimes he did manual labor for the Forest Service. When I was in the seventh grade, my parents were divorced. My mother is a Sioux, but she stayed on the Mescalero Apache Reservation even after the divorce.

My brothers and sisters and I got our first lesson in prejudice before we ever left the reservation. Because we were half Sioux, we didn't look like the full-blood Apache children, and we were teased about being different by the other kids in school. That was in the primary school on the reservation, but I still made friends and it wasn't so bad. Maybe it made me all the more determined to be a good Apache, but I don't really know that.

After elementary school I learned about another kind of prejudice. Along with other reservation kids I rode a school bus down the mountain to the little town of Tularosa and went to secondary school there. There were three different groups in the school, the Anglos, the Mexicans, and the Indians. It didn't take me long to learn that we—the Indians—were considered number three by most of the teachers and other students. Just because we were Indians, they thought we were slow. Of course, some of us still had a problem with English, and I was one of those. But that didn't mean we were slow.

I don't know how I knew it, but somehow I did know that I wasn't getting the kind of education I wanted in Tularosa. My family are Presbyterians, and after a lot of effort, I was accepted for my freshman year by a good Presbyterian boarding school in Albuquerque. I received some financial aid from the church, but I had to work in the dining room to help with the cost.

It was a hard year, but it was wonderful too. It was the first time I had known really good teaching and teachers who expected the very best work I could do. It was exciting, and I learned something I had never known before. I learned that I could do good work in a good school.

I was homesick at first, but it wasn't too bad because there was a lot to keep me busy. Besides the school work, I was getting to know white students for the first time. I never had really in Tularosa. And it was my first chance to get to know something about a city. But the real reason homesickness didn't bother me too much was that the reservation was like an anchor. I could drift, but I was tied to it, and I knew I could always get back there when I needed to.

I had only one year at the Presbyterian school because of financial problems, but I received a full scholarship for the rest of my high school education at the Bureau of Indian Affairs school in Albuquerque. It was a big letdown as far as the teaching went. I knew what good teaching was after my year in the church school, and we did not get good teaching in the BIA school.

But there was one good thing. For the first time I got to know Indians from many different tribes, and through a special school program, we had the chance to travel around New Mexico and Arizona and see other reservations. I don't quite know how to say it, but those experiences made me a better Indian. Up until then I was only an Apache. After that I was still an Apache, but I was something more.

Two special things happened while I was at the BIA school. The first was that I was talked into entering the Miss Indian New Mexico contest, and I won. I was a runner-up in the national contest that followed, and I had a chance to travel around and make speeches on Indian subjects. But it wasn't long before I realized that I was just parroting the speeches that were given to me by the organization behind the contest. They weren't my thinking or my words at all. So I dropped out. I guess I'm not a good parrot.

The other thing—the important thing—is that I fell in love in my senior year with a boy from the Pima tribe in Arizona. He wanted to get married and after we graduated I went with him to his reservation because that is where we would live. The Pima Reservation is in the hottest, barest, most forsaken part of the Arizona desert. I cried when I saw it, and I thought about my own Mescalero Apache Reservation in the cool mountains. And the poverty. The Apaches were poor, but the people on the Pima Reservation were dirt poor, poor even beyond imagining.

I was eighteen, and I know love and romance are supposed to conquer all at that age. But I knew I couldn't live there and make that boy happy. So I went home, and he stayed there.

It was good to be home, to be back with my people. And I woke up to the fact that the Mescalero Apaches aren't so poor anymore. In fact a kind of development miracle has been going on there for a number of years. I could see that much better after having visited so many other reservations. The tribe has two very good businesses on the reservation, a fine ranching operation and a logging company that give Apaches employment and make money for the tribe. And by the time I returned they were getting well into a big tourist business built around a great new luxury hotel called The Inn of the Mountain Gods. They were offering skiing, fishing, horseback riding, everything wealthy tourists could wish for.

We had good housing on the reservation now, a fine tribal headquarters, community building, gymnasium, self-service laundry, and a good new general store. We even had a museum and a swimming pool. And all this had been done without losing those things that made us Apaches.

I went to work at The Inn of the Mountain Gods. I was a hostess in the dining room, checking reservations, seating guests, giving them menus. I liked the job very much, but after I had been back on the reservation about a year, I decided that it was time to get on with my education. I didn't want to stop with a high school diploma.

I enrolled at New Mexico State University in Las Cruces, only about fifty miles from the reservation. I took a bachelor's degree in political science and history and worked for a year in Las Cruces after I graduated. Then I enrolled in a master's degree program in business administration and government at New Mexico State. I was in that program when the chance came to go to Washington, D.C., as an intern. I wanted to go and my professors saw that the internship was right in line with my studies. They even arranged for me to receive graduate credit for the work.

I've been in Washington for over six months now. I'm learning about how a big program like the National Council on the Aging works. I'm learning about big government programs. My work calls for me to keep track of all legislation having to do with older Indians and to do a health survey of elderly Indians. I have a personal goal and that is to improve my writing while I am here. I don't have any problem speak-

René Cochise walks to work, with the U.S. Capitol looming in the background.

ing, but the fact that I learned English after I learned Apache still shows up in my writing. At least I feel it does.

I don't know yet what the Washington experience will mean to me. I've met Indians here, ones who have worked here a long time, who don't seem much like Indians, not like the ones in New Mexico. I don't think that would ever happen to me, no matter how long I stayed away. I have the language of my tribe. I have the religion. I have the years of growing up on the land inside me. I have lived the customs of my people. I know who I am. No matter where I am, I am an Apache.

IN THE SEVENTH MONTH of her Washington internship, René Cochise took a two-week leave of absence to visit New Mexico. She went to the Mescalero Apache Reservation to take part in the spring ceremonies of the tribe. Then she went to New Mexico State University to take final exams for her master's degree and take part in commencement exercises.

Probably René did not think of the trip as one that symbolized her life in two worlds. It is likely that she thought of her participation in the Apache ceremonies and the commencement exercises as just the normal activities of a very busy two weeks in May.

Index